"Brent, I need to tell y

She leaned forward, not cari
word between her and Brent.

He needed to know how much he'd grown to mean to her and that God had changed her heart. As she opened her mouth to tell him of her love, she noticed someone striding down the path toward them.

"What is it, sweetheart?" Brent asked gently when she faltered. He reached over and brushed a stray curl from her forehead. Glenna stiffened and stared past him at Keith, who was leading two police officers toward them. The police were here, but where was the fire department? Flames were consuming her home and business, and the police had come?

"This man—this *convict*—is the one who started the fire!" Keith called out.

TISH DAVIS lives in Florida with her husband and three young sons. When she isn't homeschooling, she is busy writing inspirational romance. *To the Extreme* was her first published novel. Tish hopes her writing will entertain, uplift, and draw her readers into a closer relationship with the Lord.

Books by Tish Davis

HEARTSONG PRESENTS
HP426—To the Extreme
HP477—Extreme Grace
HP557—If You Please
HP638—Real Treasure

Don't miss out on any of our super romances. Write to us at the following address for information on our newest releases and club information.

Heartsong Presents Readers' Service
PO Box 721
Uhrichsville, OH 44683

Or visit www.heartsongpresents.com

Riches
of the Heart

Tish Davis

Heartsong Presents

Dedicated to my husband, Bradley. Together we have riches of the heart.

A note from the Author:
I love to hear from my readers! You may correspond with me by writing:

Tish Davis
Author Relations
PO Box 721
Uhrichsville, OH 44683

ISBN 1-59789-339-0

RICHES OF THE HEART

Our mission is to publish and distribute inspirational products offering exceptional value and biblical encouragement to the masses.

PRINTED IN THE U.S.A.

one

You're a fool, Glenna Mayfield!" Glenna muttered to herself. How did she wind up in these situations? The last thing she wanted was to interview a convict for the job opening. She had enough problems with the sanctuary without taking on this sort of headache.

The Marine Mammal Sanctuary of Long Beach, New York, was a foundation started by her grandfather Hank Mayfield Sr. He had a passion for marine mammals—all ocean creatures, for that matter—and started the sanctuary to provide a haven for hurt animals. Some were permanent residents, but most were cared for until they were well enough to be released back into the wild. At the moment they had several dolphins, otters, and a few nonmammalians like sea turtles and some tropical fish and stingrays. It was difficult to turn away any hurting creature when they had no other place to send them.

The numbers blurred in front of her as she stared at the computer screen. She didn't have to see them clearly to know what they said. She didn't have enough money. It was always that way and was only growing worse. Despite her grant from the government, which was a meager allotment, she didn't have enough capital to keep the facility running. She couldn't begrudge the amount of the allotment—every penny was a gift she didn't take for granted. Yet she needed a way to boost private donations. Her father decided long ago that he wouldn't cater to the elite by throwing fund-raising parties. Glenna also hated those affairs since she wasn't much of a people person. She liked to talk with others about her marine projects, but it was difficult to make small talk when the purpose was to extract a big fat check from the listener. So both she and her father decided they would maintain the facility through private donations from the general public. The exhibits were original, healthy, well maintained. Everyone loved dolphins, so why didn't the crowds pour through the gate? She didn't have an answer despite her many prayers on the issue. How was she supposed to keep up the sanctuary on a shoestring budget?

Her dad would tell her to do the impossible, which he thought she could do. He championed her and made her look like a superhero. Unfortunately her mother's voice spoke as loudly to her. *"Sometimes you have to walk away, Glenna. Is all this worth your effort? I don't think so!"*

"I'm not a quitter!" she said aloud, even though she heard the tremor of doubt in her voice. She stiffened, pressing her mother's words from her mind.

By looking at her, no one would think she carried the troubles she did. Though she wasn't naturally bubbly or giggly, Glenna had a pleasant disposition that reflected in her serene expression. She'd never been good at sharing her feelings—opinions were a different matter—and she believed in honesty. She was a no-nonsense person with a cap of short dark curls and a thin, athletic build. Most people considered her pretty, but she was by no means glamorous. She'd never had time for frivolous things like fashion and a social life. Her life revolved around her work at the sanctuary.

Ever since she was a child, she'd helped with the animals. Her grandfather left it to her father, who in turn would leave it to her and her sister, Crystal, one day. Both her father and grandfather had once been brilliant marine biologists.

Glenna had followed in their footsteps, learning all she could from them. She loved the sanctuary and the beautiful marine animals. They were her life.

Right now, though she didn't legally own it, the sanctuary was her responsibility. For four years she'd kept the tiny charity afloat, ever since her dad's stroke. Crystal wasn't much help. She couldn't take anything seriously, but what eighteen-year-old did? At twenty-three, Glenna felt old enough to be Crystal's mom. She was her father's primary caregiver. And she could tackle anything needing her attention—anything but the bills piled up on her desk.

She leaned forward until her head rested on her desk. A stack of bills provided plenty of cushioning. With a groan, she admitted she was at the end of herself with no obvious answer. Everyone at church was supporting her in prayer, and she knew something would break open for her. God would come through. "Lord, I know You will help me. We're sinking fast like a boat with a gaping hole. Please, Lord, show me Your answer. You've never failed me, and I know You won't now."

Glenna's prayer was one of many she'd sent toward heaven since she was a small child, though neither of her parents had been believers. The only thing that kept her sane now in her backward world was a strong faith in Almighty God. He was her comforting Father—reliable, steadfast, unchanging. There was a great difference between Him and her earthly father.

Hank Mayfield was a loving parent now, though he'd gotten off to a rough start. He'd never been a good role model or an ideal father. Glenna's earliest memory of him was of her and her sister visiting him in jail. Despite being a brilliant marine biologist, he had a history of making wrong decisions— signature forgery, embezzling, anything to keep money flowing into the mammal sanctuary so he wouldn't have to work harder. He wasn't a violent man, but he couldn't find the creativity in himself to make the sanctuary successful—so he stole from others. Throughout his years of bouncing in and out of prison, Glenna had prayed continually for him. It took having a stroke for him to finally listen. At the age of sixty, he followed Glenna's leading and took Jesus as his Savior.

Now they were rebuilding their relationship slowly.

In the meantime Glenna still had the marine sanctuary to run, and her father couldn't assist. He was bound to a wheelchair, sometimes a walker, and spent most of his time on the sofa in their tiny house at the back of the marine sanctuary's property. He wasn't physically capable of helping, and Glenna didn't want him to strain himself. He wasn't much help in the management of the business either. He'd never had any unique ideas for resurrecting their finances even when it had been his responsibility. So the job was left entirely in Glenna's hands.

If only she could find someone to work for her cheap! No one in their right mind would take on such grueling work for such little pay, though.

A soft knock sounded on her office door. Glenna rose and ran her fingers through her tousled curls. "Come in!"

Crystal poked her head around the office door. "There's someone here to see you. He says he wants a job. You better hire him. He's really gorgeous!" Her blue eyes sparkled mischievously. "I might hang around more often if he's here."

"Send him in," Glenna muttered darkly. Thinking about bills had made her almost forget about this appointment. She'd agreed to the interview only as a favor to a friend and fellow marine enthusiast, Gary Erickson. She would never consider an ex-con working for her—she'd learned her lesson often enough through her father—but this guy came highly recommended by Gary. But once he heard the amount of pay he probably wouldn't be interested anyway.

Into her office walked a tall, slender, blond-haired man about her own age. Glenna's blue eyes widened with surprise. She'd expected him to look like a hardened criminal with tattoos and tobacco-stained teeth. One look at him cut through her stereotypes like a warm knife in honey. He was nicely dressed in pale slacks and a dark button-down shirt. His hair was short and freshly trimmed, not hanging in greasy strands. If she hadn't known better, she wouldn't have expected him to have a prison record. And Crystal was right—he was gorgeous. Green eyes, the color of a grassy spring meadow, stared back at her. How many women had fallen under his control? A smile on his lips would make him look devastating. Swiftly she cleared her head of those ridiculous thoughts. Since when did she take notice of attractive con men?

Glenna ducked her head to study the papers her friend sent on the man. His name was Brent Parker—an all-American name for this all-American guy. What did he do to land himself in prison for a year? She was sure the information was somewhere on the form, but she couldn't find it. He didn't look like the criminal type. And that was the problem—looks could be deceiving. She'd best get the interview over with and send this handsome convict packing. He could only mean trouble.

Glenna looked up to find Brent frowning at her as he waited. "Sit down, Mr. Parker," she said, assuming a voice of authority. Why did she sound more breathless than she intended?

He folded his tall frame into the chair opposite her. Even as they sat at eye level, Glenna still felt considerably smaller than him. And she felt at a disadvantage.

"I see you've spent a year in a state correctional facility," Glenna said stiffly in an effort to feel in control. Again she perused the form, missing the information she sought.

When Brent didn't answer, she lifted her gaze from the paper to stare at him. His expression was unreadable—no remorse, no humiliation, no reaction whatsoever. Perhaps he *was* a hardened criminal. "Mr. Parker? You were in prison?"

"Does it also say I languished for many months in a Mexican prison cell while the bureaucrats worked out the details of my sentence? I don't suppose it mentions how I was transferred back to the United States? The bus I was on with really dangerous criminals broke down. Two men escaped. The rest of us were beaten for the guards' mistakes. I was underfed, underdressed, and treated with utter contempt. Does it tell you I've paid for my crime in full? And I will probably continue to pay the penalty throughout the rest of my life."

All this was said with very little emotion. Brent met her gaze evenly, almost with a hint of boredom.

Glenna wasn't fooled. Her gaze narrowed on his dis-passionate features. No one could speak of such things with so little feeling. She knew a storm was raging beneath the surface, but he kept it under control. Could she take a chance on him? He seemed different in both his appearance and his behavior. If she hired him, would she be sorry? That tightly leashed storm could burst through the surface with any provocation. *No,* she thought with a slight shake of her head. She couldn't make a decision based upon how she felt when she looked at him. She couldn't throw aside her reliable experience and take a chance because this man moved her emotionally. Her father taught her that second chances always led to third and fourth and fifth chances. Once the door opened, it was impossible to close. Brent Parker couldn't stay.

A niggling doubt tickled the back of her mind. The verdict she made went against everything she ever learned in Sunday school. She was supposed to help those in need and be compassionate where it was required. It was a virtually impossible task in real life. Did they have struggling marine sanctuaries in Bible days? She couldn't let her livelihood sink into nothing just to give this ex-con a chance.

Glenna gathered her composure and forced herself to remain determined. "I'm sorry, Mr. Parker. I don't think this is—"

Another knock sounded, and Crystal thrust open the door. Glenna looked at her sister in irritation.

"Sorry!" she whispered, gazing at Brent. "I don't mean to interrupt, but I thought you should know. Keith Dempsen is here, and he's snooping around the dolphin tank."

"No!" Glenna jumped to her feet and strode to the door, forgetting about Brent Parker. Keith Dempsen had no right to nose around their property uninvited. Among all the stresses in her life, he was the greatest now.

She left her office with Crystal close on her heels. Vaguely she was aware of Brent following in her wake, as well. She hurried across the premises toward her uninvited visitor. She had to intercept him before any damage was done.

Keith Dempsen was no longer by the dolphin tank. He had moved beyond the stingrays to the third pool that held two large sea turtles. She watched him staring as if mesmerized by their swimming in circles. Glenna knew he was no lover of sea life. He was probably calculating how much money he could get for the two turtles.

"What do you want, Mr. Dempsen?" she asked as she eyed

him warily. She forced her voice to remain neutral.

"Is that any way to greet an old friend?" he asked with a slow smile. Glenna was sure he expected his smile to make her weak in the knees. He was a handsome man with dark hair and even darker eyes. Glenna knew when he looked at her that he was planning his next move, and his shifty eyes missed nothing. They also revealed the lies that tripped so easily off his smooth tongue. He often hid behind dark glasses, but he couldn't hide his words. Even now he spoke falsehoods that made Glenna bristle.

"We're *not* old friends, Mr. Dempsen. What is it you need?"

"Glenna, please don't be so hostile. I'm really not your enemy," he said softly. His gentle tone almost persuaded her to relax toward him and let down her guard. Not a good idea!

"Why are you here?" she repeated stiffly, crossing her arms over her chest. She hoped he'd get the idea she wouldn't bend easily to his will. The sooner he stated his business, the sooner she could send him on his way.

"I just came by to renew my offer to buy this property. Think what a relief it would be to get it off your hands. There are no tourists. How do you afford to keep the doors open? Why, look how sickly this loggerhead is. And all you feed him is lettuce. He'll waste away."

Glenna opened her mouth to tell him to mind his own business, but Brent spoke before she could.

"That's a female green sea turtle, not a male loggerhead. They're generally smaller and are content with a snack of romaine lettuce. By the appearance of the turtles, the tank, and the water clarity, I'd say the turtles are in excellent health."

Glenna stared at Brent in amazement, her irritation with Keith Dempsen forgotten. Where had Brent learned about turtles? Then she remembered Gary Erickson had recommended him. He would have gained his knowledge from Gary, one of the greatest marine biologists along the Gulf.

"Who are you?" Keith asked, posturing himself like a prize bull at the county fair.

"He's my new assistant," Glenna answered, surprising everyone, including herself.

⁂

"I didn't mean to hire him!" Glenna groaned into her hands. After asking Brent to clean the glass in the stingray pool, she beat a hasty retreat back to her office and slammed the door behind her. She couldn't believe Keith had incited her to such irrational behavior. He was smug and arrogant, always trying to make her feel helpless. He knew the mammal sanctuary was floundering, and he planned to maximize on her struggles.

For the last three months he'd appeared every week like clockwork with an offer to buy the property. The corporation he worked for, Delta Ray Investments, owned an upscale hotel chain. They had their eye on the property for expansion in New York. The offers hadn't been reasonable, though Keith made sure she knew some of the better portions of the sanctuary would be incorporated into their architecture. It was a nice gesture, but the offered amount was insulting. They wanted to steal the ground beneath her feet.

At first Keith insisted on talking with her father since he was the legal property owner. Knowing how weak her father could be when it came to easy money, she thought they would have to look for a new home. Surprisingly he deferred all negotiations to her. Sensing that the older man was an easy target, Keith was disgruntled when he had to deal with Glenna alone. She could tell by the tight line his lips formed whenever her father refused to see him.

Now she had even greater troubles. She'd only wanted to put Keith in his place for once. But because of him she now had a convict for her assistant. She felt a twinge of guilt over the thought. She knew God wanted her to be fair to Brent. It wasn't easy for her to trust after all her father had put her and Crystal through. Crystal could accept people with a blind faith, but it was never up to her to pick up the pieces. Glenna owned that unhappy task. Thanks to her mother she looked for the dark side in every silver lining. *"Remember my words, Glenna. Men who go to jail are men you can't trust. Don't ever get involved with a convict."*

"He won't last long," she tried to reassure herself. "The pay's lousy, and the working conditions are pitiful. He'll leave before the week is over—before he can cause me any trouble." She groaned again when she realized how false her words sounded in the quiet room.

&

Brent reveled in the menial task Glenna had assigned him as she ran away to her office. He knew she hadn't intended to hire him. One look at her stony expression told him enough. She didn't want him. No one wanted him. But he wasn't one to turn down a gift tossed in his lap. Glenna Mayfield may not relish having him as her employee, but he'd make sure she never regretted hiring him.

With sleeves rolled to his elbows Brent quickly swiped away the fine coating of algae from the interior of the glass. It felt good having his hands in saltwater, working around marine life. During his years in college under Gary's instruction, he'd learned a lot. He goofed around a lot, too, and made the worst decision of his life. But he had gained an appreciation of the majesty of the ocean. It never ceased to amaze him how much detail and creativity God had put into those waters. Everything about the ocean fascinated him. It had so many intricacies. Colorful delicate corals, fierce giant sharks, playful seals, and fish of all sizes and colors. It all fascinated him, and he was so thankful to have a second chance.

His time in prison made him appreciate what he'd gained from his studies. He knew if Glenna Mayfield would give him the opportunity, he could prove himself a valuable employee. He wasn't afraid of hard work, and messing around was a thing of the past. One look around the sanctuary told him Glenna needed help. Some of the equipment needed repair, and the entire place begged a new coat of paint. No line of customers was beating down the door, but he hoped with his help things would turn around for her. They could be an answer to each other's prayers. He needed a job. She needed someone with knowledge to help her. And by the looks of that suavely dressed shark that was casing the joint earlier, Brent knew he'd come at the right time. If only he could convince Glenna he wasn't a two-bit criminal waiting to go back to jail.

Prison was an experience he didn't plan to repeat. As a poor college student he'd been broke, desperate, and foolish. Stealing then selling endangered sea turtle eggs in Mexico was illegal. He'd known the risks, but he did it anyway. And then he got caught. Taking the eggs seemed like such a simple way out of his problems at the time. It was the first time he consciously broke the law—and the last. Would Glenna try to understand? By the hardened look on her face he doubted it.

"What are you doing?" a little voice came from the direction of his elbow. Brent turned and saw that a small girl had come up behind him. She stared intently at the cloudy tank, trying to see the contents.

Brent squatted down so he was at eye level with this tiny tourist. "I'm cleaning the stingrays' house just as you probably clean your room. They're called Atlantic stingrays. Would you like to touch one, if it's okay with your mom?" He met the gaze of the girl's parent who nodded her approval.

"Please!"

Brent wiped off his hands before lifting the child to his knee. Together they leaned over the shallow pool and waited for one of the stingrays to circle near. The tan sea creatures, about the size of dinner plates, glided gracefully through the water.

"Here comes one! Now gently reach down and touch his back. Watch out for his eyes. They don't like to be touched around their eyes." Brent guided the girl's hand toward the gliding creature. Her fingers came in contact with the slick, smooth skin. The girl let out a squeal of delight.

Brent set her away from him and dried her hands with a towel. "You know never to touch a wild stingray in the ocean, right? Our stingrays here don't have a poisonous barb anymore, but wild ones still do. Stay away from them in the ocean."

"Will they chase me?" the child asked, staring at Brent with wide blue eyes.

"No. They'll swim away from you. But always watch out for them. They like to hide in the sand, and only their eyes stick out. So you have to shuffle your feet, making sand clouds in the water. The stingrays will swim away as fast as they can."

"Okay!" The girl grinned at Brent, then ran back to her mom.

Brent was filled with a great sense of satisfaction until he looked up to find Glenna staring at him. And by the frown that creased her brow, she didn't seem pleased. Brent sighed and turned back to his scrubbing. He certainly had his work cut out for him.

❧

Glenna had watched Brent with the little girl and was struck by how kind and gentle he was. He didn't act like a dangerous criminal as he taught the child about the stingrays. He could have passed for the child's father—both blond-haired and intense as they studied the stingrays together. It struck an odd chord within her and made her curious in a way she didn't want to analyze. She had enough problems in her life without adding Brent. But then again, he had been good with the tourists, and he had an exceptional knowledge of the marine life. She wouldn't have to teach him from scratch. In fact he probably knew more about the animals she housed than she did.

She strode purposefully toward him. If he was staying, it was best he understood the rules.

Brent's back was toward her, and he was vigorously scrubbing the tank; but as she drew nearer, he turned.

"Brent, I wanted to talk to you—" Before she could say more, her foot snagged on a hose stretched across the ground. She pitched forward and nearly fell, but Brent reached out and caught her at the waist. Held in his strong grasp, she was kept from hitting the ground.

Glenna stared in stunned bewilderment as Brent's green eyes gazed down at her, studying her as curiously as she had him. For a moment she imagined he might kiss her. Time seemed to stand still as he held her close and their gazes locked. She held her breath in anticipation—but nothing happened. He gave an imperceptible shake of his head, then ever so carefully set her away from him.

"I shouldn't have left the hose there," he said.

"But you didn't. I left the hose. It was my fault," Glenna argued. It was strange he would so easily take the blame.

"I'm almost finished here. What would you like me to do next?"

"Are you sure you want to stay? The work isn't easy, and the pay is lousy," she warned.

Brent shrugged. "It suits me fine."

"Well, if you're sure, I'd like you to fix all the loose boards on the boardwalk. Then clean the pumps on the walrus tank. You know how, don't you? Good." She nodded at Brent's easy acceptance of her orders. He didn't smile, but she could see his eyes sparkling. It caused a glimmer of warmth deep in her heart, but then she remembered that she couldn't allow herself to care for him. Any relationship with a con man was a mistake. For all the joyous days she had with her father, she'd had many more days of darkness. And her mother always said, *"Don't let down your guard. A man with a record is a man of manipulation."* Brent could bring just as much darkness into her life if she let him get too close.

As she walked away she called back to him, "Room and board are included. You'll stay in a small cottage next to our house at the back of the property." Under her breath she added, "And Brent, please don't make me regret this."

two

Brent tried not to notice when Crystal stuck out her tongue at her sister. Glenna lightly but firmly suggested that if Crystal had plans for the evening, then she should finish hosing down the otter house.

"She can be such a warden at times," Crystal huffed as Glenna hurried away to her own work.

"And what do you know of those things?" Brent chided gently.

"More than you think," Crystal groused. She jerked the knotted hose, and it started spraying everything with a heavy, cold mist. "Oh, great."

Brent wished she would elaborate, but he didn't want to press into matters that weren't his business. He had dozens of questions circling in his mind that didn't have answers. How bad was the trouble the mammal sanctuary was in? And if it was going under and they didn't want to sell to Keith Dempsen, why didn't they take steps to improve the atmosphere? Brent was no marketing expert, but he did know a fresh coat of paint would do the place wonders.

He had other questions about the family. Why wasn't he allowed to speak with Mr. Mayfield? The man sometimes loitered about. He seemed friendly enough and often started conversations with Brent in the evenings; but as soon as Glenna appeared, the man became silent. It was obvious she didn't want them speaking together, but why? And was there a Mrs. Mayfield somewhere in the story? Glenna seemed to carry the weight of the entire family.

He agreed with Crystal that Glenna could be heavy-handed. She gave orders as soundly as any drill sergeant. But she also worked harder and longer than anyone else. Even when he was dragging with exhaustion, Glenna still worked an hour or two more.

"I think she's more like a prisoner than a warden," Brent murmured. Crystal had gotten the hose under control and was hurrying away to the otter house. She had a date that night, and Brent knew those otters would be squeaky clean in record time. His thoughts, however, didn't stay on Crystal but returned immediately to Glenna.

She intrigued him in a way no other woman had. When he was in college he had the reputation of a flirt. He liked to tease girls and make them fall in love with him. He never allowed his own heart to get involved since he hadn't found anyone worth taking that particular risk on. So he went from relationship to relationship, never treating anything or anyone seriously. He didn't care about assignments and barely passed his classes, except for his courses with Gary. Parties were fun, but even they weren't important. Nothing held his attention for long, and nothing slowed him down until he made his mistake. And then he was brought to a screeching halt.

Brent was thankful that, when his world came to a stop, he had plenty of time to think. And he remembered words spoken by many Christians who had passed through his life. He had to get his business straight with God. So he accepted Jesus into his heart and made a commitment to value relationships more than anything else. Now that he was out of prison, it was his chance to prove he was no longer the careless boy who stepped behind those binding walls.

He hoped Glenna would give him a chance. She never knew the Brent of before—he knew she used her imagination and conjured up an ugly picture. He would utilize this time to prove to her she could trust him. She would see he was reliable and worth the risk. And he hoped he would be able to keep his thoughts on work and not on Glenna.

She was beautiful in an understated way. He liked how she shoved her hand carelessly through her thick dark curls when she was working and how she chewed on her bottom lip when she was thinking. Her blue eyes sparkled with fire when she laughed and shot icy darts when angry. She was strong, taking so much responsibility on her slim shoulders. Never did she complain or ask for help when she could handle something herself. Yet beneath that sturdy exterior was a vulnerable woman. He hadn't glimpsed it for himself—she would never allow him to see her weakness—but he knew it was there. She was like a prisoner, and her cell had no walls. Maybe Crystal was right. Glenna was the warden, driving herself.

He wanted to help her. God didn't want her to carry the burden of so many troubles. He wanted to carry it for her. And yet she insisted on doing it all herself. He wished he could take Glenna by the shoulders and tell her about grace— how God provided for all her needs and gave new chances to everyone, including him.

As Brent went on to his next task of feeding the harbor seals, he couldn't keep his thoughts off Glenna and her problem with the sanctuary. His mind went to work on making the marine sanctuary a fabulous attraction and learning center. It would draw the tourists and locals alike. It was a dream of his to share his passion for the ocean, and this was a way to do it. If only he could convince Glenna of making a few small changes here and there. He was afraid she would be insulted. Or worse, she'd ignore his suggestions because he was a convict. Well, he'd just show her what an ex-con could do. He'd surprise her and stick around until the mammal sanctuary became a success.

Brent stared at the seals as they greedily snorted and yelped for more fish. Each of the three seals measured about five feet long. Two had been rescued as pups and were too tame to be released back into the wild. The third had been rescued after a shark attack. Her tail was badly torn, and her left flipper was missing. She swam like a torpedo with its guidance system out of whack. Brent could have spent all day watching their antics, each with the playful personality of a puppy.

"Glenna must be doing better than I thought if she can afford to have her employees daydreaming on the clock."

Brent turned, not surprised to find Keith Dempsen in the small, dark room behind the seals' tank. What did surprise him was how he'd snuck in without alerting Brent.

Brent eyed him warily, taking in the dark sunglasses, immaculate suit, and cynical smile. He doubted much humor lay behind that smile.

"Is there something you need, Mr. Dempsen?"

"Actually, yes. And I think you're just the man to help me out." Again he flashed his tight little smile.

Brent had the feeling that Keith considered him beneath his class. For his purposes, though, he would lower himself—briefly—to Brent's level. Brent bristled but kept himself in check. "Go on."

"Since you're new here and, I'm sure, sadly underpaid, you might want to earn a little extra cash. We'd be doing each other a favor. All I'm asking is that you keep an eye on Glenna for me. Tell me when she leaves, what orders she makes, who she talks with. I want to know everything about her."

"Why don't you just ask her out on a date?" Brent asked, being deliberately provocative.

"I don't want to date her! I just want to know what's happening around here. She's got it in her head that I'm the enemy, and she doesn't like me near this place. It's no big deal really. Tell me a few of the common things that go on around here, and I'll pay you a few bucks."

Brent stared at Keith with a mixture of anger and disgust. One word fitly described the man. *Predator.* Sharks tearing at their food were mere goldfish compared to this man, and Glenna would be wise to steer clear of him. He was after her property, and Keith would do anything in his power to get the advantage over her—even bribe her employees. It was obvious Keith Dempsen didn't know whom he was dealing with. Brent promised himself he'd do whatever he could to protect Glenna from this man.

"I think you'd better leave, Mr. Dempsen."

"You won't help me, huh? Then you're a bigger fool than I thought. You'll go down with this dive; I promise you that. There's no future for you here, and now there's no future for you with my company. You'll be sorry for this."

"You can't hurt me. And I'll make sure you don't hurt Glenna," Brent promised. But his words went unheard because Keith had already stormed away.

❧

Glenna sat in her office, gazing out the window. With so much to be done she ought to have been hard at work, but she couldn't bring herself to do anything at the moment. Every time she set her hand to a task, Brent's image interrupted her work. It didn't help that he was so handsome. She'd worked with nice-looking men before and was able to ignore them just fine. Brent was different. He wasn't flashy or rough as she might have expected. He was gentle and kind and a hard worker. He made it very difficult to dislike him. Not that she wanted to hate him. She just couldn't get attached to him. Sooner or later he would leave, and she'd be in the same predicament as before, looking for help and trying to stay afloat.

It was a confusing situation at best. The more she got to know Brent, the more she liked him, and that scared her. So she pushed him away, acting mean and hard to show she didn't care. He never said anything when she ordered him around. But sometimes she caught a twinkle in his eyes before he ducked away. Did he know it was all an act?

A firm knock sounded at the office door, startling Glenna. Before she could answer, in strode Keith Dempsen. He closed the door behind him and marched toward her as though he already owned the place.

His charming grin was firmly in place as he slipped into the seat across from Glenna's desk. She met his gaze evenly as he studied her face. Glenna knew he saw the dark circles of fatigue under her eyes. She wished he wouldn't look at her like that—as if he knew of her troubles.

She stiffened her shoulders, squaring off for another battle. "Two visits in two days? You're becoming a permanent fixture around here, Mr. Dempsen."

"It's Keith, remember? We've been over this before, Glenna. Even though we have a few differences as far as business goes, I'd like us to be friends."

This made Glenna hold herself even more rigid. Friends— with him? She'd rather swim in a cave full of eels. Even if he weren't trying to steal the land out from under her, she would have a hard time imagining a friendship with this man. They were from two different worlds. It was easy to see by the expensive cut of his suit and the fragrance of his rich cologne that he wouldn't settle for less than the best. Glenna had rarely known the finer things in life, though she trusted God to provide for her every need. Was there a middle ground between her and Keith? It wasn't worth contemplating. He was dangerous.

"I don't think that's possible," she answered tightly. Her refusal didn't reach him.

"Glenna! Relax—I'm not going to bite you." He leaned forward suddenly and grasped her hand. "Go out to dinner with me tonight, and let me prove I'm not a bad guy."

Glenna carefully disentangled her fingers from his hold, much to his amusement. "Dinner is not a good idea," she mumbled, feeling foolish. She knew he wasn't interested in her. This man could make her blood race with anger and then have her bumbling like an idiot within seconds. The sooner he left, the better! What would it take to convince him the marine sanctuary wasn't for sale and never would be?

"What could be more important than proving myself to you?" He lowered his gaze to her lips.

"I have plans," Glenna stammered, grasping for anything to get out of the trap Keith was pulling her toward. First they'd have dinner, and slowly he would whittle away her defenses. He was a salesman—smooth and confident. She wasn't foolish enough to believe he was interested in anything besides her property.

"Plans?" He lifted his brows in unspoken challenge. Clearly he didn't believe she would have plans apart from saving her pitiful business.

"Yes, I have plans with Brent."

A tense silence filled the room. Glenna could have bitten

off her tongue for that slip even though she hadn't lied. Brent was going to help her paint the front sign.

"Do you really think that's such a good idea? We're friends, Glenna. And I care about you. I don't want to see you get involved with any unsavory characters."

Glenna wasn't taken in by Keith's quick maneuvering. No one insinuated themselves into her life that easily. "What makes you think Brent is unsavory? I haven't found anything questionable about his character." *Except that he was a criminal. But that isn't any of Keith Dempsen's business.*

"I didn't want to tell you this, but he approached me with an offer. It's reprehensible, really. Terrible. I don't know if I should tell you." He paused as though he didn't want to divulge the awful truth; yet Glenna knew it was a tasty morsel on the tip of his tongue.

"What did he offer?"

Keith sighed with a flare for drama. "He said he would keep an eye on your dealings and report your every move to me. Can you imagine? I consider us professional adults and now friends. How terrible that one of your own employees should stoop so low. It's outright betrayal. I didn't want to tell you, but I had no choice."

"I see." But she didn't.

Glenna didn't want to believe Keith. She knew he wasn't trustworthy, and Brent had done nothing in the past week to raise her suspicions against him. She'd watched him closely like a hawk circling a mouse, expecting him to make a mistake. But he hadn't. In fact, he'd exceeded her expectations.

Yet what did she really know about him? He had a prison record. That much made her cautious. He never mentioned any friends or family or personal details of his life. Was it possible he was working against her?

She rose, indicating their meeting was at a close. Keith took the hint and stood, as well, when she moved toward the door. "Let me help you, Glenna. You need my protection. Consider my offer to buy the property. Then you won't have to deal with Brent or others like him. You'll be free from all this." He waved his arm, taking in the rundown furniture and piles of paperwork. The curtains were faded. The carpet was threadbare. For the first time Glenna saw her shabby surroundings through Keith's eyes and didn't like it.

Keith took advantage of her sudden dismay. "You'll be able to seek your own interests for the first time in your life. Let me set you free from this."

Set her free? She wasn't a prisoner, though Keith must see her as one. The sincere look on his face was almost believable. But Glenna wasn't a trusting person by nature, not anymore. Her father had seen to that when he didn't keep any of his promises to her. She didn't want Keith's warnings or his protection.

"Thank you for your concern, Mr. Demp—Keith," she corrected when she caught his quick frown. "But I can take care of myself. And of course we won't entertain any offers to sell the marine sanctuary. Find yourself another piece of property for building your hotel."

Keith stepped closer and slipped his arm around Glenna's shoulders. She stiffened and tried to pull away, but he ignored her discomfort. He leaned toward her until their noses were nearly touching. "I don't think you understand, Glenna. I don't want just any piece of property. I want yours. And the harder you fight, the more I want it."

❧

Keith Dempsen must have thought he was alone as he sneaked into the mechanical room behind the dolphin aquarium. No one had followed him out of Glenna's office, and Brent knew she expected Keith to show himself to the door. Only he wasn't going directly to the door, and his detour was probably going to cause problems. Brent crept silently behind him and slipped into the dimly lit room. Only a bare bulb dangled from the ceiling, casting eerie shadows over the noisy pumps.

Pausing suddenly, Keith glanced over his shoulder. His eyes narrowed, as though he suspected someone was standing behind him. Brent froze, thinking Keith must have heard him. But that was impossible since the pumps covered his movements. He shrank back into the shadows in case the man turned unexpectedly. Watching with fascination, Brent saw him grab one of the hoses that pulled water from the dolphin tank. He slid his hand along the hose until it met the juncture into the large tank. He produced a small knife from his pocket and pierced the hose. Water spurted forcefully through the pinprick. Brent knew it wouldn't take much for the hose to rend further, and they'd have a huge mess on their hands. The pumps would fail. The water level would drop to dangerous levels in the dolphin pool as the water flooded the operations room. The cost to repair this mess alone could send the sanctuary into bankruptcy. He had to do something.

Short of tackling Keith, Brent couldn't do much. So he waited, nervously staring at the water pouring from the hose. Keith pocketed the knife, gave his handiwork a satisfied smirk, then turned. Seconds passed, but it seemed to take forever. Brent slipped out the door before Keith could see him. As Keith passed outside, Brent was waiting for him.

"What are you trying to do, Dempsen?"

Keith looked startled, but he masked it with cool in dif ference. "I don't know what you're talking about. And I really don't have time for this conversation. I'm late for a meeting."

He tried to brush past Brent, but Brent clapped his hand on Keith's shoulder. "You won't destroy Glenna. I won't let you. You asked me to keep an eye on things, and I promise I will. My eyes are everywhere, so don't think you can cut a hose without my knowing it."

Keith glared at Brent. "You can't prove anything! If anyone needs to worry, it's you. You'll be unemployed. I'll see you sent back to wherever you came from!"

Brent watched Keith make a hasty retreat. As the man ran away, Brent promised himself that no one would send him back to prison—Keith had inadvertently implied that, though he didn't know of Brent's past. Brent had made his mistake and paid his penalty, and now he was going to do his best to see Glenna set free, as well. He didn't know why he felt so passionately, except that he couldn't stand to see someone trapped in a self-made prison. He knew what God wanted him to do. Glenna needed his help, and he wouldn't rest until all this was behind her.

three

Brent hurried back to the pump room as soon as he was sure Keith wasn't going to do any more damage. By the time he returned, an inch of water covered the floor in the small room. A quick inspection told him the hose hadn't torn further, but it was just a matter of time before the pressure caused the hose to burst.

"Thank You, Lord!" he muttered under his breath. Keith had intended this little prank to ruin Glenna, but if Brent hurried, he could prevent any real harm from being done.

He shut off the pump and closed the valve that allowed water to flow into the pool. The sudden silence felt ominous. Brent hurriedly stripped away the silicone seal that held the hose to the dolphin pool.

Suddenly the door flew open.

"What are you doing?"

Glenna rushed into the room. Brent sighed. She couldn't have picked a better moment to convince herself of his guilt. Had Keith warned her about the little episode in the pump room?

"The pump is off, Brent! Why is the pump off? And where is this water coming from?" She sloshed through the flooded room to stand over Brent. He suddenly knew what a deer felt like, caught in the headlights.

"You've cut the hose! How could you?" She shoved his hands away from the hose. "I knew something like this would happen, but I didn't trust my instincts. Once a convict, always

30

a convict. My mother told me that often enough, and my father proved it true."

Brent winced, stung by her harsh words. He admitted he did look guilty, sitting in a flooded room with the damaged hose in his hands. What hurt was that she automatically assumed the worst of him. After all his hard work, hadn't he proven he was a faithful employee to her, even a friend? She couldn't see that because she couldn't see past the bars that once surrounded him.

"Keith warned me something like this might happen, but I refused to listen. He told me there would be trouble."

So Keith had planted suspicions in Glenna's mind. Brent had an even greater battle on his hands than he'd expected. It wasn't enough that she didn't trust him because of his past, but Keith was undermining him, as well. Would he ever win her trust and prove he deserved a chance?

Brent sadly shook his head, knowing he'd never convince her with words. "If we cut the hose just past the pierced section, we'll be able to reconnect it. It'll shorten some of the slack, but you'll still be able to salvage the hose." He reached past her and finished scraping the silicone.

"Pierced section?"

"Keith cut the hose. I need something—a saw—to cut the damaged section."

Glenna went to the tool chest and retrieved a hand saw for Brent. "Why would he do this? It would have killed the dolphins if it hadn't been caught in time."

"I'm sure he expected you to think it was a natural occurrence, but he didn't expect me to catch him in the act. This was probably meant to drive you into agreeing to his terms."

Glenna watched as Brent repaired the hose. Within minutes he had the hose reset and finished sealing it. "We can't afford to give the seal time to set, but I'll clamp it. That should do the trick nicely." Once the pump was back on, Brent watched with satisfaction as water shot cleanly through the hose without spilling to the floor.

Brent grabbed the mop from the corner and began sopping up the water. He knew Glenna was watching him, but she remained silent. He heard only the sound of the sloshing water as he pushed it toward the clogged floor drain. That was another thing needing his attention.

"Keith did this?" she asked finally, her words heavy with doubt—or was it disappointment?

"Yep," Brent answered without looking up.

"You saw him come in here, and you watched him cut the hose with a knife?" Now there was no mistaking her doubt.

Brent paused and pinned her with his gaze. There was no way he would cower and take the blame for Keith's deeds. Glenna didn't want to believe an ex-con was innocent. "I followed him in here. I hid behind the machinery over there." He pointed to the bulky pumps that hummed furiously. "And I watched him shove his knife into the hose. I'm sorry I didn't get a picture, but my camera wasn't handy."

"You don't have to be sarcastic. I believe you!" Glenna answered.

It didn't sound like much of an apology, Brent thought grumpily. He mopped at the water more furiously, sending a fine spray toward Glenna's legs. It gave him no satisfaction when she jumped back, hissing with irritation. If it wasn't for the fact that he needed this job, he would quit. No one wanted a warden riding his back and throwing around false accusations.

It would be just as bad anywhere else, and at least I'm doing something I love, Brent reminded himself. Taking a deep breath, he released his frustration. It wasn't Glenna's fault. Keith had misled her into believing the worst. Getting mad wouldn't make the situation any better.

He didn't realize Glenna had stepped close behind him until he swung around, knocking them both off balance. Glenna's feet slipped on the wet floor, and she let out an astonished squeak as she swayed backward. Brent dropped the mop and grabbed her around the waist before she could fall, then inadvertently brought her against the strong wall of his chest.

She stared up at him, her eyes wide with surprise. Brent felt just as surprised having her in his arms. Before he knew what he was doing, he lowered his lips to hers in an unexpected, gentle kiss. For a mere moment he allowed himself to savor the touch of her before coming to his senses.

Stunned by his own boldness, Brent set Glenna firmly away from him before she had a chance to protest. If he thought she looked surprised before, this newer shock was monumental. He hadn't meant to touch her, let alone kiss her, though he'd considered it a few times in the past week. It wasn't like him to act spontaneously. That sort of behavior could land him back in jail; yet kissing her had seemed the natural thing to do.

He snatched up the mop and attacked the remaining water. "Please forgive me for my brash act, Glenna. I won't let that happen again." He turned abruptly, refusing to meet the shocked gaze she still wore. Silently Glenna slipped out of the room, leaving Brent to deal with the water and his own troubling thoughts.

&

The next several days were a blur for Glenna. All she could think about was that unexpected kiss, though by the way Brent acted, he didn't give it a second thought. She couldn't fault his work. He was more diligent than all the other employees she'd ever had. And he to seemed genuinely to enjoy working with the animals. The only thing different was that the easy camaraderie was gone. Before the kiss, they had been cautiously building toward a friendship. Now Brent treated her with professional courtesy and a reserve that matched her own. It was her own fault. She never should have accused him of cutting the hose, even though seeing the water had been such a shock.

"I shouldn't be worrying about this. We hardly know each other. He's here today, but he'll probably be gone tomorrow," Glenna muttered, as she wiped fingerprints from the eight-foot-high aquarium. The enormous tank held a slow-moving manatee that looked like a floating stone. The only time he got excited was when romaine lettuce was tossed into the water.

"I wish he wasn't such a nice guy. It would be easier," she complained to the manatee who stared at her curiously with wide, unblinking eyes.

Glenna didn't like the wall that had been erected between her and Brent. She couldn't help thinking about the kiss and wondered if he felt the same unexpected connection she did—if "connection" was the right word. She could think of others—electricity, eruption, combustible power. She couldn't keep from being curious about him, even though she should stay away. Most of the time she could forget about his prison record since he didn't act like a typical con man.

With a sigh she sat on the bench in the observation alcove and watched the large mammal swim contentedly in the tank in front of her. He'd been hit by a speedboat in Florida, and for lack of a better facility, he'd been transported to the sanctuary once he was healed. He was old, and it was best he lived out the rest of his days in safety rather than being released back into the wild.

"God, tell me what to do about Brent. I've never met anyone like him. I know I should forget about him, but he is continually at the back of my mind. Help me talk to him."

"Talking to yourself, sister dear?" Crystal interrupted.

Glenna started, feeling self-conscious for praying aloud. "Did you want something?"

"You just got a call from Mr. Sewler. He says they won't be supplying us with any more feed fish."

"What?"

"He said they won't—"

Glenna shoved her fingers through her dark curls in frustration. "I can't believe this! What am I supposed to do, catch a ton of fish by myself every day? Did he say why?"

Crystal shook her head. "He wasn't as friendly as usual. It was sorta strange. He just said they're through working with us. And that's that."

Glenna leaned back with a groan, her mind working overtime in search of an answer. She scarcely heard Crystal change subjects and ramble on about her upcoming date that night or the fact that she thought Brent was really great or that she might even consider dating him if he'd ever ask. All Glenna could think was that her world was falling in around her ears and there wasn't a shovel big enough to dig her way out. She didn't even notice when Crystal left her alone again in the small alcove.

"Lord, Your Word says You'll supply all my needs according to Your riches in glory. I need fish. Lots. And I can't go out in a boat like the disciples did. Please, Lord, without feed I'll have to sell the sanctuary in a hurry. Please help me."

As she prayed, she knew immediately who had sabotaged her. But knowing the source of her problems didn't help her find a solution. She couldn't confront Keith, because he would deny everything. And then he would pressure her to sell. He wasn't stupid. In fact, he was the craftiest man she'd ever met. Not for the first time she wondered why he'd chosen her little piece of land to prey upon.

૨✦

When they ran out of feed fish two days later, Brent knew it was up to him to set things straight. He didn't know what he was going to do, but God would give him direction. The best place to start was down at the dock where the fishing boats brought in their catch.

Brent didn't know exactly what he was looking for as he strolled around the docks. A shrimp boat was tied off, its heavy catch evident by the hordes of seagulls hovering overhead. The gulls screeched and dove, hoping for a tasty morsel. Brent watched as the men worked, shouting orders at one another. It wasn't foreign work to him, and dozens of memories assailed him as he watched the men. He'd worked a fishing boat during his college days to make extra money— back during his days of desperation.

He moved farther down the dock, knowing he wouldn't find the information he needed with the shrimpers.

Duke Sewler had the biggest fishing operation on the dock, with fifteen boats fully loaded with equipment and crew. And from what he'd heard, Duke was a fair man and had been in business more years than Brent had drawn breath. He was a giant in his own right, and this was the guy who refused to supply Glenna with more fish.

Brent stepped on board the largest boat, feeling the gentle sway of the deck under his feet. A few of the men eyed him curiously, but none approached him or broke away from their tasks. Brent ignored their stares and strode across the deck to the helm house.

When he slid back the door, a huge, hulking man glared at him from within the small, shadowy room. He had a long white beard that hung down over his girth, and bushy white eyebrows framing his dark eyes.

"Mr. Sewler?"

"Who are you?" the man bellowed.

Brent wasn't daunted. He'd met far gruffer characters in prison. "Brent Parker. I work for Glenna Mayfield at the Marine Mammal Sanctuary."

A flicker of dismay passed over the man's face. "I don't have to explain anything to you, sonny."

"I'm not expecting you to, sir."

"I have my own pressures to deal with," the man continued. "It's not that I have no sympathy for Glenna's situation. In fact, I have the greatest consideration for her. But I have to protect my business. Delta Ray started putting pressure on me, snooping into my taxes and banking. I had no choice but to break the business I have with the Mayfields. I explained all this to the little gal on the phone."

"You're saying that someone forced you to back out of your agreement with Glenna Mayfield?" One guess who that was.

The man looked agitated, and Brent sensed the conversation was coming to a rapid close. "I'm not here to cause you more trouble, Mr. Sewler. I just want to help Glenna. She's a fair employer and a new friend of mine. I don't want to see her get hurt."

"Neither do I." Mr. Sewler coughed uncomfortably. "But my hands are tied. If I provide her with feed, my business goes under. It's that simple."

Simple blackmail, Brent thought. There had to be a way. *Lord, open another door for me so I can help Glenna,* he silently prayed. "I have experience working fishing boats. Maybe if

I donate my time you could—"

Mr. Sewler shook his head, his mighty jowls rippling. "I understand your concern, son, but I can't have anything to do with it."

Brent had to clamp his teeth together to keep back a hasty retort. Making this man angry would do nothing to help Glenna save the marine sanctuary. He had to think. He had to be smarter and get one step ahead of Keith Dempsen. But how could he? It seemed Keith had won this round. But God was on Brent's side. There had to be a way around this.

Brent stuck out his hand to shake Mr. Sewler's. "Thanks for your time—"

"You see that boat over there? The one with a black hull?" Mr. Sewler wrapped his thick arm around Brent's shoulders. "That's my nephew's operation. You tell him I sent you."

"You mean—"

Mr. Sewler nudged Brent toward the door. "Glenna's a good girl. I never did want to dump her business. Had to. Now you get outta here."

Brent thanked the man, feeling a new door had just swung wide for him. He jogged down the dock to the boat Mr. Sewler had pointed to. It was rickety and rusted and nothing compared to Mr. Sewler's fleet. Rather than working at the nets and hauling the catch, the crew sat idly—drinking, smoking, and letting the fish rot on the deck. For a second Brent thought he had the wrong boat. But, no, this was the one Duke Sewler had pointed out. Brent swallowed his dismay and went in search of the captain.

Woody Sewler was a younger version of his uncle. They shared the same broad belly, glowering eyes, and gruff mannerism. "You say my uncle sent you over here?" Woody muttered around the stub of his cigar. He sized Brent up with an ugly curl to his lip.

Brent nodded, trying to ignore the puffs of smoke gathering around his face and filling his lungs. "That's right."

"You must want a job."

"Well, not exactly. I work for the Marine Mammal Sanctuary of Long Beach, and we're having a problem with our feed fish supply. Your uncle thought you might be able to help me out."

"You work for the sanctuary? Glenna Mayfield's outfit?"

"That's right."

Woody took another puff of the cigar. "I dated her awhile back. We were real close."

Yeah, and I'm the next president, Brent thought wryly. From what he knew of Glenna, there was no way she would date someone like Woody Sewler.

"Since she and I are old friends, I'd be happy to help you out." He named a figure that more than doubled the amount Glenna had paid Duke Sewler for the same service. The only reason Brent knew this was because he'd overheard Glenna talking to Crystal about the problem.

"She can't afford to pay that much. You know that isn't a fair price."

"Times are hard. What do you expect?"

"If you cut the price two-thirds, I'll help bring it in."

Woody eyed him with new interest. "You're an experienced deck hand?"

Brent shrugged casually but didn't take his gaze off Woody. "Yeah, I worked fishing boats a few years back. I know the business."

"I won't pay you a dime. You show up at six every evening, and you're mine until we bring in the catch, usually middle of the night." Woody puffed contentedly, his eyes gleaming with satisfaction. He knew he had Brent cornered without any other options.

Brent hated running out of choices. He didn't want to work all day for Glenna and all night on a fishing boat. It was grueling work. But it meant the sanctuary would be safe, so Brent knew he would agree to anything this man suggested.

Finally he gave a stiff nod. "Fine."

❧

Glenna stared at the phone as if it were a detestable serpent. Keith was on the other end of the line, waiting for her answer to his dinner proposal. He'd offered to take her out dozens of times—the man had unending persistence—yet this was the first time she felt tempted. He said he knew who was responsible for her feed supply problems. And he wanted to discuss it over dinner. She wondered if he planned to confess.

"You won't pressure me to sell while we're having dinner?" she asked finally, knowing she had to answer him. She drummed her fingers impatiently, wishing she didn't feel like a cornered prey. There were so many things she needed to do rather than matching wits with Keith Dempsen. The sanctuary was due to open in an hour, and only half of the animals had been fed. Only half her staff had been paid. And, speaking of staff, where was Brent? He was usually working before she arrived, but he had yet to show his face. She'd begun to trust him. Maybe that was a mistake.

"It will be strictly social, Glenna—aside from one or two concerns."

Glenna wasn't sure she liked that option any better. "Fine. We'll have dinner just this once since I need to know who's sabotaging my business."

As she hung up, a blaring horn sounded at the rear delivery

gate. Curious, Glenna went to investigate. At the driver's insistent honking she swung open the gate, and in drove a truck with a giant tub of fish.

"The dolphins will feast today!" Brent called out of the passenger window.

Glenna's mouth hung open in surprise. Aside from the sparkling triumph in his eyes, Brent looked terrible. Dark circles ringed his bloodshot eyes, and he needed a shave, not to mention a shower. Where had he been, and where did the fish come from?

"Don't ask any questions," Brent ordered as he came around to her side. "Just accept that your feed fish will be delivered as before."

"You arranged this? What are you involved in, Brent?" she asked suspiciously. She wasn't ignorant of how criminals worked. They liked to buy favor. Many times her father brought home lavish gifts to make up for his weeks spent in prison. And a few times the police showed up at the door to take back the ill-gotten gains. Glenna looked outside the gate, expecting to see a squad car pull up and take away the fish. She needed the feed but not at any cost.

"I didn't steal anything, if that's what you're thinking," Brent said, accurately interpreting her expression. Glenna couldn't deny she'd been thinking such things.

A muscle worked in Brent's tight jaw. "This supply came by hard-working, honest men. And you're still going to have to pay for it. All I'm asking is that you don't ask questions and you don't talk to anyone about it. You could hurt more people than yourself if you do."

Glenna didn't understand. And, if anything, his explanation only raised her suspicions more, but she wouldn't press. Instead she'd watch him, though she hoped she wouldn't catch him in the act of something illegal. For now, she was grateful for the fish and glad Brent had come through for her. "Thank you, Brent. This really helps us. Why don't you go get cleaned up? Then I need your help. We're a little shorthanded today."

Glenna thought about Brent's surprise delivery all day as they worked together. He helped her repair and finish painting the main sign out front. Glenna could tell he was exhausted, but he didn't complain and didn't slow his pace. Neither did he confide in her. She wanted to ask him a dozen questions, but by the closed expression on his face, she knew she wouldn't get any answers.

Even when she sat down to dinner at an elegant restaurant that night with Keith, she still thought about the mystery encompassing Brent. Normally she would be uncomfortable and self-conscious in such a fancy place, but she was so distracted by her musings that she hardly noticed her surroundings.

"I'd like to think you're daydreaming about me," Keith said with a slow smile that could only have been practiced dozens of times for effect.

Glenna blinked in consternation, chasing away her thoughts about Brent. "I—I was thinking about the sanctuary."

"Shall we dispense with the business so we can focus on the social aspect of this date?" Keith asked before taking a sip of his wine.

Glenna reached for her glass of water. "This isn't a date, and you know that," she responded quickly. She had to admit he looked handsome tonight and was making every effort to be pleasant. The least she could do was be civil with him. "Tell me who's sabotaging my business."

"You get right to the point, don't you?" When she didn't

answer, he continued. "You're not going to like this, but don't say I didn't warn you." Keith put down his glass and stared at her intently with his dark eyes. "It's one of your employees."

"No, you must be mistaken," she said, though in the back of her mind she wondered who the responsible party really was. Before Brent showed up with that load of fish, she thought she knew. Now she wasn't sure of anything.

Keith shook his head. "Glenna, it's Brent Parker. I warned you about him. He's nothing but trouble."

"Why should I believe you?" she retorted. "I have no reason to suspect Brent of this. He's the most loyal of all my employees, few as they may be." Even as she said the words she couldn't help the doubt that crept in. Would he purposely ruin one of her business agreements? What would he gain by it?

"There's more. I'm sure he lied about this on his resume, and with you being so trusting, I have to tell you. He has a prison record, Glenna. You need to stay away from him before he causes more harm to you. And it may not be your fish supply he attacks next time."

Keith was checking up on her employees. The thought didn't give her any of the comfort he intended.

"Promise me you'll fire Brent. I can help you find someone to replace him."

The arrival of their meal saved Glenna from having to answer. The food looked delicious, but she had no appetite for it and barely tasted what passed her lips. She unconsciously pushed her food around her plate, wishing she was back at the sanctuary so she could talk to Brent.

Keith didn't seem concerned with her silence. "You realize I think you're a beautiful woman and I'd like to get to know you better. If it weren't for our business dealings, I think we'd get along quite well together."

Glenna tipped her head to the side, eyeing Keith doubt-fully. "I'm surprised to hear you say that. I'd never consider myself your type." She could easily picture him with wealthy, sophisticated women. He'd like someone who worried about pedicures and fitness trainers or what time they needed their chauffeur to drive them to the country club. Glenna didn't fit in that scene. She didn't have time for it, nor did she want it.

"You might change your mind once I kiss you," Keith sug-gested, giving her another of his slow, melting smiles.

"Excuse me?" Rather than warming to him as he intended, the thought of kissing Keith turned Glenna cold. After Brent's kiss she couldn't imagine being close to another man. She may not know what to think of Brent and his dealings at the moment, but his kiss was forever imprinted on her mind. The thought of Keith kissing her was repelling. And like the open book she was, her expression must have conveyed her thoughts.

"I've gone about this all wrong, haven't I?" Keith asked as he leaned forward and studied Glenna's face. Her eyes narrowed suspiciously as she expected another smooth maneuver from him.

"The look on your face tells me I've really messed up," he said with a deep sigh. "But I can't blame you, can I? I've gone after your property like a bulldog goes for a bone. And I haven't been fair to you. I don't want you to think of me like that. We should have met under different circumstances. Then you wouldn't suspect my every move. Can't we start over? If it weren't for business, do you think we could be friends? I'm just a man, Glenna, who works for a corporation. It's only a job to me. We could forget about the marine sanctuary and any other circumstances. Forget all business dealings for a minute. Could you like me? Is it possible we could be friends? I'm not your enemy, Glenna."

Friends? Glenna thought of Keith as a predator, a leech, the man who wanted to steal her property. If she put aside all the circumstances as he suggested—ignored his intentions to profit at her expense—could she see him as someone who might be interested in her? Glenna looked at him, trying to see him for the first time. Keith Dempsen, potential friend? She couldn't be sure on that score, but he was correct on the other hand. Yes, he was just a man—and a very handsome one. But it was too difficult to separate how he handled business from his personality. Weren't they one and the same?

Glenna swallowed, suddenly unable to meet his gaze evenly. She didn't like the personal turn their conversation had taken. This was new territory that made her feel unsteady and uncomfortable, off balance, like a bird treading across quicksand.

"Glenna?"

She raised her gaze and hesitantly met his. "I'll have to think about it."

four

I've made a decision," Crystal announced. The baby otter she was holding stared at her curiously, then proceeded to wiggle free of her grasp. Crystal gently pulled the little fur ball back.

"Hold him still," Glenna ordered. "I'll never get his nails trimmed if you don't stay focused."

"I'm going to start dating Brent," Crystal continued as though Glenna hadn't interrupted.

Glenna's hands stilled as she stared at Crystal in dismay. No attractive Christian man within a fifty-mile radius was safe from Crystal's attention so Glenna shouldn't have been surprised at her sister's decision. Brent was handsome and charming, besides being a hard worker and an unexpectedly good listener. It shouldn't have taken two months for Crystal to pin her attention on Brent. But Glenna didn't like hearing about it, though she wasn't sure why. The fact that he was an ex-criminal with the possibility of a future transgression didn't bother her as much as it should have. Her friend who had recommended him assured her she could depend on him. Could she trust him with her sister? It didn't feel right. She didn't want Crystal dating him, and she certainly didn't want them kissing each other.

"Don't you think he's too old for you?" she asked, grasping for something to discourage her sister.

"Because he's your age?" Crystal teased. "Five years doesn't seem that significant to me."

"I don't think it's such a good idea," Glenna murmured. "I

hardly think Brent is your type."

"Why? Do you think he's your type? You're always working, and I've never known you to have a social life. It never occurred to me that you might be interested in him. But if you'd rather go for him—"

"It's not because of me!" Glenna protested. "Has Brent shown any interest in you? Flirted with you?"

Crystal shrugged. "Naw, but that's what makes the chase even more fun. He doesn't even know I'm interested. Yet."

Glenna shook her head in dismay. She and her sister were so different. Glenna was old-fashioned and believed any relationship between a man and woman should evolve naturally without the woman shamelessly pursuing the man. Crystal was bold and sometimes aggressive. She likened patient waiting with growing moss. It was just one of the many things Glenna and Crystal disagreed on. Glenna wanted to be a good example to Crystal, but the younger girl didn't often pay attention to reason. Instead she could be flighty and flirty. She was a sweet-tempered, vivacious girl—Glenna couldn't complain with how she turned out. Living without a mother had been hard on both of them. Glenna had become both sister and mother to Crystal for the past ten years. When their dad went to prison the final time, their mother decided to leave; she couldn't take the pressure any longer. Glenna and Crystal had been sent to live with their father's aunt until he was released. Though they always had some form of adult supervision, Glenna had taken it upon herself to look after Crystal. She hadn't done a bad job, but sometimes the responsibility weighed heavily on her.

Many nights she lay restless, praying she was doing things right. Sometimes the bitterness would try to creep in. It wasn't fair that she'd been left with so much responsibility—

given to her by two irresponsible parents. But God was always guiding her and loving her. *"The Lord is my shepherd, I shall not be in want. He makes me lie down in green pastures, he leads me beside quiet waters, he restores. . ."* Glenna's mind faltered over the next part of the psalm. Did God really restore her soul? She knew the Word was true; yet she felt as if His peace was just out of her grasp. Maybe if she worked harder, did a little more, she'd be able to reach it.

"Crystal, be careful. I love you, and I don't want to see you get hurt," Glenna answered finally, resigning herself to Crystal's insistence. What else could she say without adequate reason? If things got out of hand, she'd have to talk to Brent. But for now she'd trust Crystal to do the right thing.

Crystal gave Glenna an impulsive hug, squeezing the wiggly baby otter between them. The little animal squeaked and tried to climb up Crystal's shirt. She giggled and pressed a kiss to the furry head. "Glenna, you're the best!"

⁂

Watching Crystal flirt with Brent was a nauseating sight. To Brent's credit he was very patient with the girl while keeping her at arm's length. It was like watching a strange battle. Crystal would move forward; Brent would parry her attack, then retreat. Crystal was relentless in her pursuit of him, turning on her full charm. The more Glenna watched, the more frustrated she felt. It wasn't possible she was jealous, was it? No! She'd never been jealous before in her life, and certainly not of Crystal. Regardless of what she was feeling, she didn't like seeing her sister throw herself at Brent. It was undignified.

Glenna frowned with displeasure as she watched Brent and Crystal working together with such easy camaraderie. As they cleaned the stingray pool, Crystal splashed him several times, and Brent rewarded her with his tolerant smiles.

"Their relationship bothers you, doesn't it?" her father asked as he came up behind her.

Glenna stiffened. "Dad! Should you be out here? You're taking it slow, aren't you?"

"Glenna, honey, stop parenting me. I'm just fine, and it's good to get a little exercise. Why don't you tell him how you feel?"

"I don't know what you're talking about," she answered casually, turning back to the sheaf of papers in her hand. The numbers blurred on the page as she tried desperately to bring her wayward thoughts into focus. How could her dad believe she felt anything for Brent? Her mother had given her enough warnings about men like him. Give her five minutes, and she'd have fifty reasons to stay away from Brent.

She could see her dad wasn't fooled. He gave her one of those looks that said, "Try another line because I'm not biting on that one."

Glenna met his gaze defiantly before giving a sudden sigh of defeat. She couldn't fool her dad any more than she could fool herself. "Oh, who am I kidding? No, I don't like how Crystal has attached herself to Brent's side, and I can't figure out why. He's a nice guy and good-looking, but he's a—" She came to a halt, staring uncomfortably at her father.

"He's an ex-con, just like your father," he finished for her. "It's all right, honey. I can tell what you're thinking without your saying a word on the matter. This isn't really about Brent or his past. It's about me."

Glenna held up her hand before her father could start the self-recriminations and endless apologies. She'd heard them enough over the years, and it didn't matter anymore. She'd told him numerous times that all was forgiven and she loved him. "Dad, it isn't about you. This is something I have to figure out for myself."

"We're going to have a serious talk one of these days. You have a lot of junk locked up tight that you refuse to let go of. It's keeping you from really living. God doesn't want you to live in such bondage to the past—to your fears and resentment. And neither do I, honey. God wants you to be free. You have to get it out."

"Dad, I'm not sure I can. I don't know how." She looked at him miserably. "Can we change the subject?"

"That's right. We were talking about Brent," her father said with a sudden grin. "I think he's a fine boy, and I'd be pleased if one of my daughters ended up with him. He has some great ideas."

"What sort of ideas, Dad?" Glenna asked.

He patted her shoulder affectionately. "Good ones! And honest," he added when she gave him a suspicious look. "Have you ever talked to him about why he went to prison? You might be surprised. He isn't as bad as you suspect, and he has some brilliant ideas to turn this place around. That boy has a real love for the business."

Glenna frowned at her dad's enthusiasm. Warning bells were pounding in her ears, and so were her mother's words. *"Keep the cons apart! If you don't, you'll be sorry."*

"Dad, are you sure you and Brent should plan moneymaking ventures?"

"But—"

"Just hear me out. He's fresh out of prison. Neither of you should bring temptation into the other's life. Does that make sense?"

"I understand perfectly, Glenna Andrea Mayfield. You're afraid that Brent and I haven't changed at all, that we might mess up again. Well, you're wrong. And I won't allow your fears to keep me from building a friendship with Brent Parker. He has some outstanding ideas for our mammal sanctuary. I choose to support him, and I like him!"

⋙

Brent didn't know what he'd done to earn the formal treatment he was getting from Glenna. She only spoke to him when necessary, and her smile rarely reached her eyes. Sometimes he would catch her looking at him, but she would quickly avert her gaze each time. He wished she would come out and say what was bothering her rather than making him crazy with her silence.

Brent knew her stiff behavior could be a result of a couple of things. It was possible Keith Dempsen had poisoned her further. The slick panther had been hanging around Glenna more than Brent liked. Her father didn't like it either, but he trusted Glenna to handle the sanctuary's business. Brent wanted to argue that Keith had more than business on his mind as he slowly tore down Glenna's defenses. It wasn't just the property he was worried about.

Crystal might be the other reason Glenna was angry with him. The girl was in obvious hot pursuit, and Brent didn't know how to let her down easy. She was nice and spirited. He enjoyed her playful humor. But he had no desire to entertain a relationship with a precocious teenager. A lifetime had passed since he had been that age, and sometimes he couldn't relate well to Crystal and her endless chatter. He'd much rather spend his time talking with the serious yet lovely Glenna.

Brent knew God had given him an opportunity to confront Glenna when he found her sitting alone, eating lunch. It was a cloudy afternoon that had brought dozens of tourists inside to avoid the storm. Though the marine sanctuary was partially outdoors, most of the people crammed inside to avoid the random drops of rain. Glenna must have ducked outside for a moment of privacy to enjoy her sandwich.

When she saw Brent coming, she quickly gathered her stuff to go, but he blocked her hasty retreat. "You're avoiding me, and I'd like to know why. Have I done something?" He crossed his arms over his broad chest and stared down at her, silently daring her to escape.

He watched the storm clouds pass through Glenna's eyes as she returned his steady gaze. He wished she would smile at him. When she allowed herself to relax, her smile could light up a cloudy day.

A smile was the last thing Glenna had to offer. "*Have* you done something? You and Crystal play around all day. She's reckless and young, and I expect her to act like a silly teenager—but not you, Brent. Why do you tolerate her flirting?"

"So you're concerned with my love life. Is that it?" Brent asked, keeping all emotion from his voice. If he didn't know better, he'd say Glenna was jealous of her sister. She showed every symptom of it, but Brent knew that was too much to ask for. She'd made her feelings about his past abundantly clear. She'd never like him because of where he'd been.

"Your love life is your own business, Brent, but I'd appreciate it if you'd stay away from my sister. She can be impulsive, and she's not always practical," Glenna answered stiffly.

"So if you're not concerned with my love life and who I date, then you won't mind if I start seeing you." He took a measured step closer.

Glenna's mouth dropped open and her eyes widened, as a bright flush crept up her neck. Brent couldn't help feeling amused by her reaction.

"I know you don't want to give me a chance," Brent continued when Glenna had trouble answering. "Is it me or my past that bothers you so?"

"Brent, I—I don't think that's a good idea. You're an employee here, and we should leave it at that."

Brent let his arm drop to his side as he stepped back, giving her plenty of space to escape. "You're right. Forget we ever had this conversation, Glenna. I'll leave you alone. And just for the record, it has been Crystal pursuing a relationship, not me. I like the girl as a friend, but I haven't encouraged anything more between us. She's not the Mayfield girl I'm interested in." At Glenna's look of dismay, Brent held up his hands in surrender. "Don't worry. I'll keep things professional just as you want it."

❧

Glenna ran away from Brent as if hounds were nipping at her heels. She'd forgotten her half-eaten sandwich since her appetite had fled with his unexpected declaration. He wanted to date her and not Crystal. She couldn't even consider such a thing.

Of course you'd consider it, she chastised herself. She'd done just that ever since his unexpected kiss. And that's why she didn't enjoy seeing Crystal flirting with Brent. She didn't like her wayward heart that was unaccountably drawn to him. She knew it was dangerous to get involved with a man like Brent, but her heart didn't want to listen. She'd have to pray harder to stay immune to his charms. Given his past, he probably knew how to manipulate her emotions, but somehow she would stay ahead of him. She wouldn't make the same mistakes her mother had made.

Glenna ran from Brent and straight toward Keith without realizing it. He'd followed a group of tourists into the dolphin observatory. Glenna didn't notice him until she was passing by and he suddenly gripped her about the waist.

"What? Oh, Keith."

He looked closely at her face, and a frown puckered his brow. "You look a little flushed—upset. Everything okay, Glenna?"

When had he come to care so much for her feelings? Glenna wondered. Last she knew he was ready to rip away her livelihood without a concern, and now he cared about her agitation?

"You come here almost every day, Keith, and I doubt you drop an offering in the donation box each time you pass it."

"I usually sneak past it with my hands in my pockets," he admitted with a grin. It was a devastating smile that probably brought weakness to most women's knees. "Otherwise it would cost me a fortune to see your pretty face."

That line was a little hard for Glenna to swallow. She was about to challenge him on it when she noticed Brent heading toward her. She couldn't handle another confrontation with him, especially in front of Keith.

"Can we call a momentary truce? I need to get out of here now!" She tried to brush past him to find a quiet place to think, but Keith stopped her.

"I'll take you for a short drive." At Glenna's suspicious glance, he added, "Think of it as a peace offering. I won't even mention the property."

Glenna considered his offer. If she stayed, there was every chance she'd have to face Brent again, and she wasn't ready to do that. "Just a short drive," she said, relenting.

"Anything you say," Keith said with a smug smile firmly in place. He rarely missed anything, and Glenna was sure he knew the reason for her anxiety—maybe not the *exact* reason, but certainly its source.

Keith ushered her to the gate where his new red sports car was parked. Glenna slipped into the cool leather of the passenger seat, feeling grungy in her T-shirt and overalls. As usual Keith was immaculate in a dark pressed suit.

"Where to, fair lady?"

"I don't care as long as it's a short drive." Glenna leaned against the headrest and closed her eyes. It had been a brash decision to take off with Keith. She hadn't planned on hopping in his car and allowing him to whisk her away. He would surely badger her about selling the property even though he promised not to.

Keith sped away from the sanctuary. Glenna sank lower in her seat, enjoying the comfort of the leather. Soft music played on the radio, lulling her to sleep.

Glenna hadn't realized she'd fallen asleep until the car stopped and Keith gently shook her shoulder. She blinked hazy eyes at him, trying to reorient herself. It was dark, and they seemed to be in some kind of underground parking garage. "Where are we?"

"I've brought you to my home in Brooklyn."

five

Glenna stared at Keith in disbelief. It would have been easier to accept if he'd told her he was her long-lost brother. "Please say I didn't hear you right. I am *not* in Brooklyn. And this is *not* where you live. I'll wake up in Long Beach, and you'll still be bothering me for my land."

"Come on up, and I'll show you the place. It has an incredible view of the city. At night with all the lights, it's quite spectacular." He reached for the door, but Glenna refused to move. She crossed her arms over her chest and stared at him.

"What's wrong, Glenna?" Keith asked with an edge to his words.

"I don't know you that well, and I'm certainly not going up to your apartment. What were you thinking?"

"I was *thinking* you wouldn't want to go to a fancy restaurant wearing work clothes, and I *thought* you'd be more comfortable in the privacy of my home. I assure you my intentions were honorable."

"Well, you thought wrong," Glenna snapped. "You shouldn't have brought me here. I thought we were going for a short drive."

"To me this is a short drive."

"Is this just another ploy? I'm still not willing to sell the land."

"Do you think that's what I'm after? Hasn't it occurred to you I might be interested in something other than your property?" Keith glared at her, then rifled his hand through his dark hair.

"And what might that be?" Glenna asked. He'd offered to be friends, but she thought that was a ruse. Had she been wrong?

"You really don't know, do you?" Keith asked, relaxing against the seat. He reached out and tweaked Glenna's nose. "I'm interested in *you*."

Glenna said nothing.

"Are you sure you won't come up?" he asked, his words low and persuasive.

"Very sure." Why did her voice sound so strange? The car suddenly felt warm and way too cramped as Keith sat inches away, staring at her in the dim light.

"I need to get something. Will you wait right here for me?"

Glenna nodded. "I'm obviously not going anywhere."

Keith returned within a few moments carrying a small, thin box, long enough to fit a pencil inside. He slipped behind the wheel and turned in the seat to face Glenna. "Here." He placed the velvet case in her hands.

"What is this?"

"Open it and find out."

Glenna slipped off the lid and peered inside. She hoped it was a pencil, but no, it was a thin gold bracelet. She took it out of the box and held it up to the light. Tiny dolphins had been etched into the gold. It was lovely—and totally inappropriate. She dropped it carefully back into the box and handed it to Keith, but he refused to accept it.

"I can't take it," she stated. "It isn't right for me to accept expensive jewelry from you. Besides, it seems strange."

"Strange? What if I told you it's a cheap trinket from a costume jeweler?"

"Is it?"

Keith shrugged. "No. But it shouldn't matter how much it cost. I want you to have it. Remember—you said we could be friends, and sometimes friends buy each other gifts."

"I said I'd consider becoming friends. This isn't an appropriate gift, Keith."

Keith cocked his head to the side and studied her; then a smile tugged at the corners of his mouth. "Does that mean you'll accept a different sort of gift?"

Glenna flushed, feeling like a crab in a trap. "I didn't mean that—it's just—"

Keith grinned as he turned in his seat and started the car. "Relax. I was just teasing. Now let's get you a hamburger and drive back to Long Beach."

They stopped at a fast-food restaurant and opted to eat in the car. Once her stomach was full, Glenna found herself watching Keith closely. He could be witty and charming when he wanted, though she still felt cautious of his every move. He hadn't mentioned Delta Ray one time, but everything he said seemed to have a hidden agenda. He was always plotting to take the property away.

Glenna silently berated herself for getting into this situation. She'd had business dinners with Keith, but never had she met him in such informal circumstances. If it hadn't been for her reaction to Brent, she wouldn't have gone with Keith. Why had she been so afraid of Brent? He was a nice man, and she was beginning to trust him despite his past. She shouldn't have panicked.

"Do you like mountain climbing?" Keith asked suddenly as they sat watching the traffic.

"What?" His question jerked her thoughts back to the present.

"Do you mountain climb?"

Glenna shook her head. "I've never actually seen mountains. The coast has always been my home."

"What about waterskiing? Snorkeling? Scuba diving? Tell me what you like."

Glenna shrugged, taking a sip from her soda. "I don't water-ski. Snorkeling is okay, but I rarely have the opportunity. Scuba diving reminds me of work. That's how we maintain some of the tanks. Why are you asking?"

"I just want to know you on a personal level." Keith turned in his seat to look at Glenna. "I like fast cars and loud music. I travel because of business, rarely because of pleasure. I like huge parties where I can mix with the rich and famous—hoping someday to be one of them," he added with a sheepish grin. "I think I'm well on my way."

Glenna knew she was different from Keith, but now it was glaringly obvious. She liked simple things. She didn't doubt he worked hard, but for different reasons from hers. They had nothing in common. So why was he so intent on spending time with her?

"Why are you doing this—the gift, the attention? We're nothing alike, and I know you see it as well as I do. What is this about, Keith?"

Keith's gaze narrowed briefly before a slow, award-winning smile covered his face. She had seen a fleeting glimmer of something, but it passed too quickly for Glenna to identify. "Still not sure about me, are you? Let's just say you intrigue me. My mother has a flair for collecting unique things, and I believe I've inherited her tastes. Can't it be enough that I'm interested? Why do you suspect my motives?"

Because you've been trying to steal my property for as long as I've known you, she retorted silently. Wasn't it possible he'd developed an interest in her despite his business dealings? Delta Ray had sent him to buy the property, but that had nothing to do with his personal life.

"I think you'd better take me home," Glenna said finally, wishing again she'd confronted her feelings for Brent rather than running away. She didn't want any man to think of her as a unique thing to add to his collection.

⁂

Brent didn't like seeing Keith Dempsen hanging around Glenna so much. He was like a black-tip reef shark looking for innocent little fish to prey upon. He hid his dangerous mouthful of teeth behind a seductive smile and his aggression behind smooth politeness. Glenna might be dazzled, but Brent wasn't fooled. He knew Keith was after the property to turn it into a high-rise luxury hotel for Delta Ray Investments. Brent thought Glenna was too smart to fall into such an obvious trap, but maybe Keith had charms Brent wasn't aware of. He could only pray God would open her eyes to the truth before something went wrong. And he wished God would open her eyes to the truth of how he felt for her.

It was scary falling in love for the first time. Admitting it wasn't easy. Feeling jealous of Keith was worse. He was falling in love with Glenna. It was too bad he couldn't choose the object of his affection. Loving someone who ran away from him was a hit to his ego. Dozens of women had claimed eternal devotion to him, but Glenna wasn't so open with her admiration. In fact, he was happy with just a smile from her. This probably served him right for being such a heartbreaker in his youth. He'd proudly avoided love's snares, much to the sorrow of others.

Every day he watched Glenna work. She often laughed and smiled; yet he sensed her tension even when she seemed happy. He wished he could wipe away all her worries. He knew how financial problems ate away at her joy. She always chewed her bottom lip when deep in thought. It was easy to read her emotions because they reflected so clearly in her eyes. He'd seen the disapproval she had for him when he first arrived at the sanctuary without her saying a word. And now he saw something different in her eyes when she looked his way. It wasn't love, but it appeared to be something like curiosity. He knew he shouldn't put his hope in something so small; yet he couldn't help himself. He'd nurture her curiosity into affection if she would give him a chance—and if it was the Lord's will. She would see he wasn't some two-bit criminal looking for the next gas station to rob.

Brent was surprised a few days later when Crystal ran up to him and gave him an impulsive hug. She pressed her blond head against his chest and squeezed him tight around his waist. He was glad Glenna wasn't around to watch how her sister threw herself so easily into his arms. It would be another black mark against his character.

"Brent, you have to go! Please say you'll come with us. It'll be so much fun since I've never been on a yacht before. Please say yes. Please?"

Brent couldn't help feeling fond of Glenna's younger sister. He'd do just about anything to make the Mayfield girls happy. "Tell me what I'm agreeing to."

Crystal batted her eyes prettily at him. He had no doubt this was how she got her way with everyone. Any man would be easily wrapped around her little finger and not even complain.

"Keith Dempsen just invited Glenna out on his company's private yacht. It's huge! I don't think she would have accepted, but I told Keith I'd like to see the yacht, too. I made a real pain of myself, and finally Glenna said the only way she'd go was if I went with them. But I don't want to be a third wheel. So I want you to go with me, and it'll be a double date."

Brent didn't like the idea of either Glenna or Crystal being alone with Keith. Whether it was on a yacht or at a business dinner, he knew Keith was trying to manipulate Glenna. He continually tempted her with his wealth, showing her the difference between their lifestyles. He'd heard the invitations Keith made, coercing Glenna to meet with him. Once he appeared at the sanctuary with a property assessor. The only way she could make him leave—aside from calling the police—was to agree to another dinner date. Crystal told him about the many instances Keith tricked Glenna into meeting with him. Keith brought up questions of the sanctuary's public record, tax issues, even tourist complaints. And Glenna had to find a way to deal with each thing. This time she wouldn't have to face Keith alone. Brent would be happy to go with her and Crystal on Keith's yacht.

⋙

Even Brent was impressed with Delta Ray's corporate yacht. He'd spent several weeks on a yacht a few summers back so he was familiar with such a vessel. This was a Viking forty-three-foot convertible yacht, decked out with every modern convenience. Keith walked through the salon as though he personally owned the boat, pointing out the finer features of the vessel. He showed them the posh leather seating, modern media equipment, and of course the loaded wine rack. Brent hoped Keith didn't plan on sampling the wine since he'd have to man the helm.

Keith offered the ladies something to drink. Both selected soda and ignored the wine, to Keith's apparent disappointment. He neglected to offer anything to Brent. Brent knew it was a deliberate slight, but he said nothing. Once Keith had Glenna and Crystal settled comfortably on the white sofas in the salon, he left them to go to the helm. Brent followed him, like a dog sniffing out a fox.

Keith frowned as Brent watched him ready the boat for their outing. He flipped on the radio and turned the dial. Nothing but static filled the air. Next he switched on the global positioning system. He made several adjustments to the delicate instrument, and Brent saw immediately that Keith didn't know the first thing about boating. Locating the ignition, Keith twisted it. The engines roared to life.

"Listen to that motor hum. It sounds like a race car," Keith said with satisfaction.

"Twin diesel engines," Brent corrected quietly. After watching Keith fiddle with the control panel like an infant, he knew he needed to stick close. But Keith had other ideas. He obviously didn't like anyone staring over his shoulder and picking out his glaring errors.

"Hey, Brent, make yourself useful. Grab those lines so we can go." Keith pointed to the ropes securing the yacht to the pier. Plenty of deckhands were waiting to help them cast off from the marina, but it seemed Keith wanted to put Brent in his place.

Brent gave a casual shrug, then wordlessly climbed from the helm and stepped to the dock. Keith revved the engines impatiently. "What's taking you so long, Parker?"

"That's fine. I can be a servant and not a guest on this little voyage. Anything to keep a close watch on Dempsen," Brent mumbled to himself as he loosened the ropes that secured the yacht to the swaying wooden dock. He didn't really care what he had to do as long as he could stay close to Glenna. Keith hadn't mentioned the property yet, but that had to be the only reason for the outing. He was toying with Glenna and pushing her limits until she would finally give in and sell. No one ever mentioned the little deeds he'd played a part in, like tampering with the pumps or blacklisting the feed supply. Glenna may have overlooked those things, but Brent hadn't. He had a promise to keep. No one would hurt Glenna Mayfield.

With a firm nudge Brent pushed the bow of the boat away from the dock then hopped on the back deck before he was left behind. He knew Keith would have been thrilled to leave Brent standing on the dock. He'd have more opportunity to bend Glenna to his will without any wary eyes watching him.

And Brent planned to watch Keith's every step.

He knew firsthand how prison guards surveyed the prisoners. They observed, missed nothing, anticipated everything. And that was to be his job on this outing. Keith didn't know the first thing about boats, and he had an abundance of self-esteem. It didn't make a good combination for a safe joyride.

"Pride goes before destruction." Brent knew from personal experience that the verse was true. He hoped in this instance that Keith wouldn't crash until Brent delivered Glenna and Crystal safely back to shore.

The waves were about four feet and choppy, not the best day for an outing. Keith wasted no time getting away from the marina. The boat should have been able to handle the waves without any problem, but Keith was pushing it too fast. Below the helm in the salon, Brent had no doubt the girls were feeling every jarring wave. He tried to mention this to Keith, but Keith didn't want to listen.

"I'm the captain, and you weren't invited to come along, were you?"

Rather than feel indignant, he only felt more worried. It

was too big of a boat for a beginner, and Keith wasn't seeking help. It was more important for him to look good in front of Glenna. Brent knew better than Keith that she wouldn't be impressed with vain showmanship.

Ahead of them in the channel were several smaller boats, all heading for the open water. They moved at a steady clip, producing very little wake. Unfortunately Keith wasn't following their example. He plowed ahead, mindless of everything around him.

Brent held his tongue as long as he could, but Keith showed no inclination to change his course. "You're coming up on those other boats too fast!" Soon they'd be upon the unsuspecting boaters.

"Would you get out of here? I don't need your help!" Keith growled. He then reached out and grabbed the throttle. Finally the boat slowed.

Brent wanted to argue that any novice should seek help the first time out on the water, but he said nothing. Instead he climbed stiffly down the ladder to the aft deck. As his feet hit the floor the boat lurched severely. Keith had just dropped the engine speed to avoid running over the other boats. Brent wasn't surprised when the sliding door behind him opened and out stepped Glenna and Crystal. Both looked perplexed and worried.

"What happened? One minute we were sipping our colas, and the next minute we were knocked off the sofa."

Brent almost grinned at the picture of Glenna sliding to the floor in surprise. But this was no joking matter. Keith shouldn't be at the helm of any boat. "Your boyfriend needs a few boating lessons. Why don't you tell him to turn us around and head for home?"

Glenna's brow puckered. "He's not my boyfriend, and you

know that! He said Delta Ray was getting ready to put another offer together for the property. I wouldn't have agreed to this if Crystal hadn't poked her nose in the middle."

"And now we're all stuck on a boat with a captain who can't drive it."

"Brent, do you know something about boats? Can't you help him before we all drown?" Glenna asked.

That was the problem. He wanted to help, but Keith wasn't interested. "Keith's throne is made for one, and he doesn't like company."

Just then the boat lurched forward again, throwing everyone off balance. Brent kept his footing, but Glenna was thrown against him. Brent's arms closed protectively around her and held her easily against his chest. She stared up at him, her wide eyes watching him trustingly. Trust? That was a new emotion for her.

"Why didn't you catch me, too, Brent?" Crystal whined. She'd tumbled across the deck and was rubbing her tender elbow. Brent would have helped her up, but she scrambled to her feet before he could offer.

"I'm going back in," Crystal announced, shouting into the wind. "If I have to roll around the boat, I'd rather be inside where the cushions are soft." As Crystal ducked back into the salon, Brent drew Glenna to sit beside him near the rear rail.

"You doing okay?"

Glenna nodded, giving him the thumbs-up signal. "As long as Keith doesn't sink us!"

Keith seemed to be handling the boat okay for the moment. Brent didn't like sitting at the back of the boat where he couldn't see what they were coming up on. And he didn't trust Keith's judgment. He would have moved where he could watch, but he didn't want to leave Glenna alone. As Keith hit a wave particularly hard, she bumped against Brent's shoulder. To keep her steady, he wrapped his arm around her shoulders and held her gently to his side. Glenna didn't complain; instead she snuggled in closer.

Brent tried to hide his surprise. This was what he'd prayed for, that she'd accept him. She was beautiful with her dark curls blowing around her face. She didn't worry about the wind or her hair as she smiled up at him.

Carefully, while gauging her reaction, Brent laced his fingers with hers. It was such a simple act; yet when she didn't pull away it was as rewarding as a first-prize trophy. Brent's heart sang praises at the huge progress such a small act meant. If only they were together under different circumstances. It wasn't easy for Brent to relax knowing Keith insisted on captaining alone with no experience.

Suddenly the blast of a horn rent the air. Both of them jumped at the bone-jarring sound.

"Not good," Brent ground out. He doubted Glenna heard his words. He untangled his fingers from her suddenly tense grasp.

"What is it?" Glenna shouted. The wind grasped her words, but Brent knew what she asked. Unfortunately he didn't have a ready answer—only a suspicion.

Again the horn blared with deafening ferocity.

Keith was in trouble.

Brent scaled the ladder to the helm, and his worst fears were confirmed. He paused, mesmerized by the enormity of the danger they were in. "Dear Lord, help us!"

Bearing down upon them was an enormous oil tanker. Dozens of yachts could fit on the ship's decks, leaving room for crew and equipment. They wouldn't take serious notice of a tiny pleasure vessel. And Keith had placed the tiny yacht right in the tanker's path.

Panic loosened Brent's tongue and spurred him into action. "What are you doing? You're going to get us killed! That tanker is loaded with fuel!"

Keith did nothing but keep their boat on its dead-end course. The tanker saw them, but the ship's captain could do little to avoid the tiny yacht, so they sent out another warning blast.

"You can't impress Glenna when she's dead!"

Keith threw a baleful glance over his shoulder. "He has plenty of room to pass, and I'm obviously on my side of the channel. Just because he's big doesn't mean he owns the whole ocean."

"Are you insane?" Brent stepped forward, praying again, "Dear Lord, help us!"

Keith protested, but Brent shoved him firmly away from the wheel. With the wind and the tanker, the air was filled with noise. Men on top of the enormous ship had rushed to the rail and were waving frantically. Grimly Brent took hold of the wheel and gave it several sharp turns to the right. The wheel spun loosely in his hands, but the boat quickly obeyed the new course.

He didn't know Glenna had climbed up to the helm until he felt her hand on his shoulder. "Are we going to make it?" she called into his ear. Her voice quavered.

Brent nodded without turning around to comfort her. There was no time. By the grace of God he'd get them out of the tanker's way without capsizing them.

In less than a minute the tanker would have been upon the yacht had they stayed where Keith had left them. The sound of the enormous engines was overwhelming. They were so close Brent could see water splashing against the black hull as the ship passed. The passengers on the little yacht stared in awe as the giant crawled through the channel mere yards away.

The wake that followed the oil tanker was a three-foot wall of water. Brent expertly steered the boat to avoid being tossed like a hapless toy in a bathtub. Still the luxury yacht rocked on the waves, jarring its occupants. Glenna clung to him to keep from being thrown from the helm as Brent clutched the wheel.

"Hey! Don't knock us off the boat, Parker!" Keith growled as he grasped the railing to keep from pitching over the side.

Brent didn't bother glancing in Keith's direction. He was more furious than he'd ever felt. In an effort to control his churning anger, he focused on slowing the yacht and steering clear of all other vessels. Keith never should have invited Glenna and Crystal on the boat.

As the danger passed, leaving them swaying gently with the waves, Brent prayed a silent *thank You* to God. Gradually his nerves calmed. He breathed a sigh of relief when Glenna's arms slid around his waist, and she gave him a quick hug.

"Thanks, Brent."

If he hadn't intervened when he had, the joyride could have turned out much differently.

❧

It was a solemn group that returned to the Marine Mammal Sanctuary that night. Glenna was wrapped in her own thoughts, replaying every move Brent had made. The others were equally quiet. Even Crystal was subdued, and her lack of tittering dialogue was noticeable. Keith was the only one interested in carrying on a conversation. He repeatedly complained about Brent's overreaction to the situation, but

Glenna couldn't help thinking Brent had saved their lives. He'd been cool and collected as he navigated the little boat away from danger. Once Brent took control of the situation Glenna knew they would be okay. He didn't have anything to prove, and he didn't try to impress her as Keith had—foolishly, she might add. And unlike Keith, Brent had very little to say about the situation. He looked grim and even angry, huddled in the backseat of Keith's car. Several times she glanced back at him, but his stony gaze was turned to the window. Glenna couldn't blame him for being mad, though she didn't understand why Keith had lost control. She was so thankful Brent had decided to join the outing. She didn't like to think what may have happened if she and Crystal had been alone with Keith when the tanker came through.

Brent was no stranger to things of the sea. Glenna wanted to ask him where he gained his knowledge of boats. There was so much she didn't know about him. They worked together on a daily basis and had developed an ease between them, even though she held herself apart. Maybe she could open up a little. Of course she could trust him; yet it was so hard when her mother's warnings were racing through her mind. Why didn't Crystal have these problems? True, Crystal had been much younger when their mother had left, and she probably didn't remember as much as Glenna did. She was so different in the way she handled people. It was easy for her to tease Brent as though they were lifelong friends. Glenna frowned at the thought. She didn't like Crystal's flirting.

She, too, liked Brent—probably more than she should. She didn't feel so mistrustful of him; yet there were so many unknowns. It was easy for Crystal to open conversations and dig into people's lives. Glenna had a harder time getting to know others. She was naturally reserved and didn't like anyone pressing into her personal life without invitation. That was probably why she found it so difficult to ask Brent about himself. It was another example of how she'd been affected by her mother.

As Keith pulled the sports car to a stop, Brent quickly unfolded himself from the cramped backseat. Crystal squirmed out of the car and darted toward the main gate of the sanctuary. Once everyone was out, Brent lingered near Glenna like a protective big brother, eyeing Keith warily. The two men squared off, putting Glenna in the middle—each wordlessly challenging the other.

Keith made the first move as he stepped forward and put a possessive arm around Glenna's waist. He glared at Brent with open hostility. "Don't you have seals to feed or sidewalks to scrub? Glenna and I have something important to discuss—away from the hired help."

Brent visibly bristled but didn't lower himself to Keith's insults. Instead he leveled a questioning look at Glenna. She stepped away from Keith's grasp.

"This isn't about buying the property, is it, Keith? I've told you it's not for sale," she said with a tired sigh. She didn't like being stuck in the middle of their male posturing.

Keith grunted with exasperation. "No, it's not about the property. I don't care about the sanctuary. I want to talk about us!"

Glenna's eyes widened. She took an unconscious step back toward Brent, and he put a protective hand on her shoulder. Keith nearly growled at the gesture.

"Brent, I think you'd better let us talk alone," she said apologetically.

He didn't move, staring down at her uncertainly. Glenna let out a sigh. "Please." At her insistent tone Brent stepped away, allowing his hand to drop from her shoulder. He gave a last long look at Keith before leaving the two alone.

Once Brent was out of earshot, Glenna turned back to Keith and waited impatiently. After taking the afternoon off, she had a lot of work to do. This conversation was probably another of Keith's attempts to manipulate her though she had no idea what he intended to tell her. She hoped it had nothing to do with going on his company yacht again. She'd had enough of boating to last her awhile.

Keith stared down at her with his dark eyes. He wore a smooth smile that made Glenna uneasy. She tried to take a step away from him, but Keith grasped her hand. "You know I work for a successful and prestigious corporation. I've worked hard to gain the position I have, and I make a lot of money. I've gotten to this place on my own with no one's help but my own sweat and blood. Around the office they call me Mr. Conglomerate. Even the chairman doesn't have the acclaim I do. But now that I've arrived at the top I've realized something." He paused, his warm gaze on Glenna's upturned face.

His pause was ominous, and Glenna knew there was more to this conversation than she first suspected. She swallowed, feeling suddenly nervous.

"What have you realized?" she croaked.

Keith stroked her knuckles with his thumb. "I've learned that I want to share this success. I don't want to be alone anymore. What do you say, Glenna? Are you willing to become Mrs. Conglomerate?"

Glenna frowned at him in dismay. "Are you asking me to marry you?" She couldn't have been more astounded. Surely this was a joke and someone was about to pop out with a camera and yell, "Surprise!"

"I'm asking you to think about it. There's no pressure, and I don't want you to answer right away. I just wanted you to know what my intentions are."

She would never marry him. He didn't share her faith, and she certainly didn't love him. After all their business meetings and her repeated refusals, how could he think she would agree to such an offer? A marriage proposal was the last thing she expected from him.

She hadn't given marriage and her own future much consideration, except to know she never wanted the kind of relationship her parents had. Her mother must have loved her father to marry him and have his children. But life hadn't been a fairy tale, and everything changed for the worst when her father went to prison that last time. Everything fell apart. Glenna remembered what it felt like to be abandoned by both her parents. Her mom and dad had never had a marriage built on faith, and Glenna knew she wouldn't make the same mistake. She wouldn't marry someone just because he offered her security. Marriage without God in the middle was no marriage at all.

"Keith, I won't—"

Keith held up his hand. "Glenna, save your answer. I can see you don't want this, but don't reject me yet. Maybe I'll be able to persuade you to see things my way."

•

six

Brent sighed in frustration but refused to complain. A hard day in freedom was better than a good day in prison. And through the mercy of God he had many days of freedom ahead. If only Glenna was around to share in this day.

Keith had called another meeting with her. He was continually trying to persuade her to sell the property. And he was trying to convince her to marry him. The predator snatched as much of Glenna's time as she would allow. Who could tell what sort of dangers he exposed her to when she left the sanctuary? Brent didn't like it. He didn't trust Keith's motives, and he felt overly protective of Glenna. Unfortunately he didn't think Glenna wanted his protection any more than she seemed to want his love. But he worked harder anyway, doing everything he could to make things easier for her.

Brent sighed, feeling heartsick. What was he going to do about her? He loved her, and he couldn't change that. Regardless of how he prayed, a wall stood between them that he couldn't scale on his own. Glenna sat behind that wall, and she wasn't about to give him access no matter how he tried.

In the middle of his frustration he found an ally. Mr. Mayfield understood his daughter better than she probably realized, and he wanted to ease Brent's confusion. At first Brent didn't willingly divulge anything to the man, but Mr. Mayfield let on that he knew Brent was in love with Glenna.

74

It was a relief to share his heart's burden then with someone so understanding. Mr. Mayfield knew what it was like to pay the price for mistakes. And he understood Glenna's reluctance to trust. He explained that Glenna had been hurt deeply as a child because of her parents and had difficulty letting go of those hurts. He wanted nothing more than for Brent to help set her free with God's help. He felt Glenna needed someone she could believe in, who would take care of her because she'd taken care of everyone else for so long. She needed to be loved unconditionally even when she couldn't return that love at first.

"Where's Glenna?" Crystal demanded, slipping up behind Brent. He was sitting in Glenna's office going over the orders for medicine and special organic foods.

"She's in a meeting with Keith Dempsen again." Brent frowned. A glimpse at his watch told him she'd been gone most of the day.

He didn't realize he was crumpling the papers until Crystal laughed.

"You've got to be joking!"

Brent gave the girl a sharp look. "What?"

"She has you tied in knots, doesn't she? How'd Glenna get so lucky to have you fall in love with her?" Crystal pouted prettily as she fluffed her blond hair. Then she shrugged. "I guess that's okay. You and I make better friends anyway. Does Glenna know you love her?"

Was he that transparent? "You don't know what you're saying," he grumbled, turning back to the order forms. He smoothed out the creased paper.

"I can help you. I know all about my big sister—what she likes, what makes her happy, what—"

Brent knew those things, as well, but he wasn't about to

reveal that bit of information to Crystal. The fact that he'd made it a personal mission to learn everything about Glenna was no one's business but his own. "You can help me by not talking about this anymore. What Glenna does with her private life is none of my concern. Making the sanctuary profitable is my only worry. Nothing else."

Not easily put off, Crystal laughed at his stiff treatment. "That's all right, Brent. It can be our little secret. I won't tell Glenna if you don't want me to, but I think it's a shame you're hiding it. She needs your love. You'd be good for her."

Just as Crystal rose to leave, Glenna burst into the office. Her cheeks were flushed with excitement, and her blue eyes glittered brilliantly. "Come quick! Down to the beach! A green sea turtle has washed up. He looks like an albino."

"Is he hurt?" Brent asked.

"I don't know! Just come, okay?"

They raced down the path from the sanctuary to the beach where a grayish turtle lay at the water's edge. Brent guessed it weighed about a hundred and fifty pounds by its size, but it didn't look too good. The thick flippers were motionless, and his nose was buried in the wet sand. Several things were wrong with the animal, Brent noticed at once. Fishing line was tangled around three flippers. His fourth flipper—the right front one—was missing entirely.

Crystal hung back while Brent knelt opposite Glenna beside the turtle. "Have you seen a turtle like this before? He's so pale."

Brent nodded as he checked the turtle's vitals. He was alive—barely. "He's a Kemp's ridley. This is what I studied in college."

"He?" Crystal asked, peering over Brent's shoulder. "How can you tell?"

"See how long his tail is? Males have noticeably longer tails than females. Can you get some scissors, Crystal? He's badly tangled in fishing line. I've seen this before. It can be really dangerous for the animal. And bring the truck. We could carry him back, but it wouldn't be easy. We have to get him back to the sanctuary and fill him with some food and antibiotics. Glenna, can you get his rear flipper free?"

"You sound as if you've done this before," Glenna commented as she tugged at the tough line.

Brent flushed, realizing he'd stepped in as expert supervisor of the rescue mission. As his employer, Glenna probably didn't appreciate taking orders from him.

"I learned a lot under Gary. We did this sort of rescue many times." He looked up to find Glenna's curious stare resting on him. Her gaze held his, asking him questions her lips wouldn't form. Brent's hands stilled on the turtle's back as he returned Glenna's stare evenly. Was that wall beginning to crumble? He wanted her to ask him questions and learn he wasn't as bad as she imagined. He needed the opportunity to show her how far God had brought him in the last two years.

"Brent?"

"Yes, Glenna? What is it?"

"I didn't spend all day meeting with Keith Dempsen. He gave me the formal inquiry from Delta Ray. Instead of spending the afternoon with him as he wanted, I came here to the beach. To think. I just thought you should know," she finished with an awkward shrug.

"Why was it important to tell me?"

"I've just been wondering about some things. And I wanted to ask you a question."

Brent held his breath, waiting for her to take that first

important step. Everything else slipped into the background as they gazed at one another. Brent forgot about the turtle and the incoming tide that made his pants and shoes salty wet. He could see the pulse beating nervously at her throat. When her hands fluttered with uncertainty, Brent wanted to groan aloud. *Lord, help her ask!* Then she would see he wasn't the hardened criminal she suspected.

"I was wondering—are you, well, what I mean is, did you—?"

"Just ask, Glenna," he coaxed.

"Was it horrible in prison?" She quickly looked away as though ashamed to have brought up such a delicate question.

Brent stared at her, dumbfounded. He thought she would ask the reason he was sent to prison. He hadn't expected this question. Didn't she want to know he was a changed man? He had plans for a future and knew God wanted to bless his life. But this was a beginning, and he had to remain thankful for every small step.

"It was exactly what I deserved for breaking the law, so I really can't fault any discomfort I suffered. I'm never going back," he added, watching her closely.

"How can you be so sure? My dad said that a thousand times." She unconsciously trailed her fingers over the back of the turtle's smooth shell. Brent was glad her question wasn't an accusation; she really was curious about him. The stones of her private wall were coming down.

"God changed my heart. I broke the law because I was desperate, and I didn't care about anyone but myself. I even got Gary in trouble with the Mexican government. I went to jail and paid the price, but that wasn't enough to change me. God had to build a new heart within me. He took my heart of stone and gave me a heart of flesh. That's how I can be sure

I won't go back to prison. I have no desire to break the law. Do you believe me?"

Before Glenna could answer, Crystal drove the pickup onto the beach. She tooted the horn as she pulled closer, breaking any closeness that had developed between him and Glenna. He swallowed his frustration and turned his attention back to the sea turtle.

Between the three of them they got the turtle onto the truck and drove him back to the sanctuary. He was thankful the trip was brief, because the Kemp's ridley's condition was weakened. It was a miracle he was even alive with how badly tangled he was, not to mention being at a disadvantage with only three fins.

After they arrived at the marine sanctuary, they took the turtle to one of the treatment rooms that contained emergency medical supplies. They wheeled the gurney holding the turtle to the center of the room and snapped on the bright light overhead.

Something was wrong.

Brent glanced around the room, feeling uneasy. He sensed that someone was watching them. It was a peculiar feeling and rather ridiculous since patrons often watched them through the large windows as they worked on injured animals. But this was different. Brent glanced over his shoulder at the window, but no one was there.

"I'm giving him an injection of antibiotics now, and we'll wait for the vet to get here and do the rest," Glenna announced as she filled the syringe. In the meantime Crystal cut away the remainder of the fishing line while Brent checked the turtle for additional injuries. He seemed in pretty good condition aside from the missing flipper—and being exhausted.

"Brent, what is it?" Glenna asked, watching him with a frown.

Once again Brent felt that odd sensation and checked behind him. No one was there, but he knew they were under observation. Someone was lurking just out of sight, watching their every move, and it made Brent uneasy.

"Can anyone get into this room, Glenna? Or only the staff?" Once again he checked over his shoulder to find no one there.

Glenna eyed him curiously. "Only the staff. I always keep it locked." She looked around the room, and her gaze fell on an open drawer. "I didn't leave that open. Did either of you?"

Both Crystal and Brent shook their heads. Someone was messing around with the sanctuary again—little threats that mounted into giant warnings. Someone wanted the Marine Mammal Sanctuary out of business, and Brent didn't need a Ph.D. to know who that was.

Glenna crossed to the drawer and yanked it all the way open. "No!"

"What is it?"

"The animals' medicine is gone! Everything in this drawer—it's gone! Who could have done this?" she groaned. She swung around and stared at Brent.

Brent knew who would do it—Keith Dempsen. He'd do anything to undermine Glenna and force her into selling the property, even if it meant stealing a few bottles of medicine.

He wanted to take her in his arms and promise everything would be okay—even with this happening. She was striving to keep the sanctuary open, and Keith Dempsen was working against her every moment to close it. But through the grace of God they would beat Keith at his own game.

"It doesn't matter, Glenna. We have enough medicine to get by, and we can order more. Right now let's take care of this turtle."

It was advice he needed to follow himself. Brent clenched and unclenched his fists in anger. It didn't matter what Keith did because God was on their side. Each day they would fight until they won the battle. They couldn't let Keith Dempsen and Delta Ray destroy what they'd worked for.

The sound of metal hitting the floor made everyone freeze.

They turned to find a pair of scissors on the polished white tiles.

"How did—?"

Glenna's question was left unfinished when a dark-clad figure slipped through the exit. Brent forgot about the injured turtle and raced after the stranger. The man ran quickly. He was dressed in a black T-shirt, jeans, and stocking cap. His boots pounded the floor as he ran from Brent through the sanctuary. *He knows the property as well as I do,* Brent thought as he chased the intruder.

The stranger dodged tourists as he ran past the dolphin tank, through the indoor seal observatory, and out the back door. Brent nearly caught him when he reached the otter habitat, but the man slipped between exhibits. He darted behind the pump room and burst through the rear emergency exit that led onto the beach. Brent tried to catch him, but the guy was too fast.

Dusk was descending, casting brilliant colors across the sky. Brent followed the path down to the beach where he must have gone.

The man had disappeared.

"Impossible! He can't just vanish!" It was as though the stranger had been a figment of his imagination. He saw no invader on the beach. Catching the thief would have stopped the bizarre things that kept happening at the sanctuary. Brent sighed in frustration, wishing he hadn't failed.

He turned to find Glenna trudging through the sand toward him. "Did you see where he went?"

Brent shook his head in frustration. "He must have circled back somehow. I don't know how he could have gotten away." He turned back to the beach, searching the horizon for the dark-clad figure.

Unexpectedly Glenna slipped her fingers into Brent's hand and turned to him, pleading with her eyes. "I wish these things didn't keep happening, but I'm so thankful you were there. You always help me when I need it the most."

Amazing how her softly spoken words made everything bright!

"Should we go report the theft?"

Glenna nodded. "I've already called. The police should be here any moment."

❧

Once the police left after taking their statements, Glenna allowed Brent to lead her down to the beach. They walked along the water's edge, where the waves roared toward the shore, only to lap gently against the sandy barrier. Glenna stopped to unlace her shoes and slip them off. She tried not to think about the intruder. She couldn't do anything about him now. He'd stolen some medicine—she was thankful he didn't take it all—and Brent was right. They would be okay with the supply they had, and she could order more. But where that money would come from, she had no idea.

Glenna didn't want to worry about her troubles. If she turned off her thoughts for a few minutes, everything would be put on hold. She liked nothing more than to feel the sand beneath her toes as the water swallowed her feet up to her ankles. It reminded her of being a carefree little girl who could run and play as she wanted. No troubles. No intruders. The sand felt coarse to her bare feet, and Glenna realized it had been too long since she'd taken a simple walk on the beach.

Too many other duties demanded her attention and time. She couldn't drop everything to pamper herself. How simple life would be if she could forget all her responsibilities at the sanctuary for a time. Sometimes she wished she didn't have to worry about the business; yet she knew her dad would never sell. There had to be another way.

Keith wanted to marry her, "solving" all her problems. She indulged him by meeting with him to discuss the property. She knew it wasn't wise to ignore an opponent. Yet he always turned the conversation to marriage. She didn't trust him and couldn't believe he thought she might consider his offer. But he was a smooth salesman who used so many tactics it left her bewildered. Someone at church had mentioned she should seek legal support, and this latest instance with the intruder convinced her it was a good idea.

"Who do you think took the medicine?" she asked, though she was fairly certain of the thief's identity.

Brent shrugged. "I have my suspicions, but I honestly don't know."

"I wish it never happened. Now I have another problem to deal with."

"But you don't have to deal with it alone," Brent answered firmly.

When Glenna turned to tell Brent she appreciated his support and how sorry she was for not trusting him in the past, a stabbing pain shot into the bottom of her foot.

"Brent!" She clutched at him and lifted her foot, feeling like a hot fire poker had been forced into her arch. Two long, black spines were wedged into the tenderest part of her foot. She couldn't see the spiky round creature in the water, but she knew she'd stepped on a sea urchin.

Tears flooded her eyes with the sudden intense pain. She tried to pull the spines from her foot but nearly lost her balance. "Brent, I've stepped on a sea urchin, and my foot is stinging!"

"Oh, no! I didn't see it. Here—I'll help you." Unexpectedly Brent scooped her into his arms, picking her up out of the water. She wrapped her arms around his neck and pressed her face into his shoulder as he lumbered across the beach the way they had come. Now there was no leisure in his pace as he rushed back to the sanctuary.

"It hurts! I can't believe how bad it hurts!" she cried.

"You'll be fine." Brent grunted as she sucked in a sharp breath. "I've got you, and I won't let you go."

Despite the pain radiating through her foot, Glenna let herself relax in Brent's arms, thankful he was taking care of her. She could have hobbled back on her own, but she liked Brent holding her close.

Rather than taking her to the marine sanctuary, Brent followed the narrow path to the Mayfields' small home. As he was trying to adjust Glenna in his arms so he could reach for the knob, the door swung open.

"Saw you coming from the window," Mr. Mayfield stated grimly. "What happened?" He was in his wheelchair and pulled himself back out of Brent's way.

Glenna winced at her father's pinched, worried face. "I'm okay, Dad. Just a little accident," she said through gritted teeth.

"I need to get her to the sofa," Brent said as he carried Glenna through the doorway. Mr. Mayfield pointed toward the den.

In the den Brent stepped around the coffee table and lowered her to the couch.

"It's still burning!" Glenna cried. She hated her weakness and couldn't help the despised tear that trailed down her cheek. When she reached to rub at her foot, Brent stopped her hand.

"Don't touch it! You'll only make it hurt worse. We need to put ice on it to ease the pain."

"I'll make an ice pack," Mr. Mayfield offered. "I need something to do. I can't stand to see her cry—it makes me feel bad," he grumbled as he left the room.

Brent sat carefully on the edge of the couch. He leaned over Glenna and caught the tears that slipped unbidden down her cheek. "I know it hurts. Please don't cry. It makes me feel bad, too, to see you cry, and I can't take the pain away."

"You know how this hurts?" she sniffed.

"It's probably like a jellyfish sting. When I was a kid I got in a fight with a man-of-war, and the jellyfish won, of course. We went to the beach during a holiday break, and I had an unpleasant surprise—just like you." He grinned wryly. "But talking about it doesn't make this pain any easier to bear."

"I don't think talking makes any pain easier to bear."

She knew by the set look on Brent's face that he wanted to challenge her statement. She didn't like to talk about her problems—God could deal with silent complaints as well as those voiced loudly. Obviously Brent didn't agree. She knew he'd press her until she talked about her past and the things that held her back. He'd probably do it gently with her best interests at heart. But that wouldn't make the pain any easier.

Leaving it buried was safer and more manageable. "Is Dad coming with the ice?"

"You should talk about anything that bothers you, Glenna, whatever it is. You know I'm a good listener."

She returned his gaze stubbornly. Whether or not he'd listen wasn't the issue. She was afraid that if she gave an inch, the whole dam would crumble. Besides, no one could change the past. Her mom wasn't coming back, so what was the point of telling Brent anything?

"I'm bringing the meat tenderizer, too," Mr. Mayfield called out finally. "That's how we used to treat these injuries."

Glenna breathed a sigh of relief when her dad came back into the room. He wheeled himself across the tile floor to the sofa and placed the ice pack against Glenna's throbbing foot. She let out a sharp hiss at the intense pain ripping through her arch. Brent shot her a look of sympathy.

"Do you have any antiseptic spray? It'll ease some of the throbbing ache. I need some water and clean cloths, too."

"You don't want the meat tenderizer?" Mr. Mayfield asked, shaking the canister at Brent.

"Ice is the best treatment," Brent said quietly as he bent over Glenna's feet to inspect her injury closer. She had two small punctures, and her arch was a dull purple color.

Brent turned Glenna's face toward him. He checked the temperature of her skin with the back of his hand against her cheek. "Are you breathing all right?"

Glenna frowned in confusion. "Why?"

"Sometimes people go into shock when an accident happens. Do you want me to call an ambulance? It will take them some time to arrive. I could probably drive faster to the emergency clinic."

Glenna winced as she set her foot back on the sofa. "I'm

breathing okay, and I don't want to go to the doctor. The ice will help, won't it?"

"It will minimize the pain."

Mr. Mayfield returned again with a pail of water, a sponge, and a bottle of antiseptic spray. Brent took the things from him and set to work ministering to Glenna's wounds. He placed Glenna's foot in the pail and wrung out water over her ankle with the sponge. "I don't see any poisonous spines left in your skin. The irritation should diminish quickly with the ice." He patted her skin dry, then applied ice to the affected area. Glenna had to admit she did feel better as the pain lessened.

She laid back against the couch, trying to focus on Brent's gentle touch and not on the discomfort. Her eyes drifted closed as she forced herself to relax.

"I'm sorry this happened, Glenna. Thank the Lord it wasn't any worse," Brent said softly.

"I feel like a nuisance. My mom always said I was a pain. She didn't like to take walks with me on the beach," Glenna admitted with a sigh. Slowly she relaxed with Brent's ministrations. Getting hurt and having Brent help her made Glenna feel less cautious.

"You're not a nuisance," Brent assured her as he finished.

"It feels much better, thank you." She punctuated her words with a yawn.

She silently thanked the Lord for Brent and his quick thinking. He knew just what she needed. He was good at taking care of her, and she trusted him more than anyone else, surprisingly. It was something she needed to think about. . . later. Her breathing grew steady as sleepiness overtook her. Brent's touch had been so soothing, and she knew she was safe and warm and cared for.

"Maybe we could take another walk sometime?" Glenna mumbled without opening her eyes. She wasn't sure if she heard Brent's answer or imagined it as she drifted off to sleep.

"I would walk around the world for you, Glenna Mayfield."

seven

Something had changed between Glenna and Brent since the sea urchin accident. Glenna couldn't pinpoint exactly why she looked at Brent differently, but she did. She didn't know how she ever saw him as a wayward convict, a man doomed to repeat his mistakes. He was an honorable, sensitive man and too handsome for her peace of mind. Somehow along the way God had changed her thinking. It was subtle but so different—and it confused her! It went against everything her mother had taught her.

Aside from her emotional turmoil, business was picking up. Brent had suggested changes—mostly cosmetic—and more donations were starting to trickle in. It was amazing what a fresh coat of paint could do! But something was still missing. They needed something spectacular to lure the crowds, but the solution eluded Glenna. If she was going to save the marine sanctuary, she needed to figure it out—and fast.

She decided to take the question to her dad.

"Brent and I have discussed this many times," her father answered when Glenna asked his opinion. "He says we need Veero."

"Veero? I was talking about another government grant. We could file another petition—"

He shook his head. "There are no more grants—not for us at any rate. They've refused our last two petitions. But Veero will help us."

"Veero? What's Veero?" she asked.

"Veero is the solution to saving this sanctuary. I thank the Lord often for Brent and his great ideas."

"Dad, what's Veero?" Glenna asked again.

In answer her father moved over to the coffee table and scooped up a large rolled sheet of paper. Carefully he unfurled the paper across the table. Glenna peered at the picture over her father's shoulder.

"Dad, it's beautiful!" Glenna was surprised at the meticulous pencil drawing of a beluga whale. It was drawn so well that she could even detect a glimmer of humor in the creature's eyes. Where had the drawing come from? And what did it have to do with Brent's ideas for the sanctuary?

"This is Veero!" he said triumphantly.

"Dad, how is this drawing going to save the sanctuary? I don't make the connection."

"The whale, not the drawing, is going to help us," her father said, as though he were explaining it to a child. "Veero is a small whale who was injured a few years ago and couldn't be released to the wild. He needs a new home. We can bring Veero here, and he'll pull in the crowds. It's very simple."

It didn't seem nearly so simple to Glenna, but maybe this was the solution she was looking for. "How will a new acquisition make money rather than cost us money?" she asked.

Her father looked up from the drawing and smiled. Glenna listened to her father's explanation, thought for a few minutes, then cautiously agreed to give Veero a chance.

⁂

To move Veero from Galveston, Texas, to the Marine Mammal Sanctuary of Long Beach would be a stroke of genius, Glenna decided. Veero wasn't just any whale—he was a glossy white beluga with a vibrant personality. She knew he'd make a dramatic difference. Everyone who visited the sanctuary would love the antics in the dolphin tank. Veero would bring his own charm. She was glad to admit Brent was right.

Veero was under the jurisdiction of the university but was being temporarily housed at a private facility that didn't want him. He was supposed to be moved to a zoo in California, but they changed their minds once they realized new housing had to be built to hold him. Veero was homeless, and an enormous private grant was available for anyone willing to take him. It would require a lengthy boat ride for him to travel from Texas to New York, but that would give them the needed time to prepare a facility for him.

Gary Erickson, Brent's former professor at the university, sanctioned the transfer and invited Brent, Glenna, and her father to make the trip to Galveston. They received the necessary approval from Brent's probation officer and arranged to leave immediately. The sooner their "star attraction" was in his new home, the sooner the sanctuary would benefit—not only from the private grant but also from the interest Veero would generate. Money was tighter than ever, and even though Glenna was able to pay the bills, each check she wrote put her one step closer to shutting down the sanctuary. It was a risky move bringing in another exhibit, but the grant more than compensated for their expenses.

A joyous reunion took place on Gary's doorstep when they arrived. He and his wife, Chloe, seemed thrilled to see Brent again. But everyone was anxious to visit the whale, so they climbed into the van and headed for the private facility. During the ride no one could get a word in edgewise as Brent and Gary exchanged stories about Veero. They promised Glenna she'd fall in love with the white whale at first sight.

Veero was a beautiful beluga, Glenna admitted as she

watched the whale swim circles around the tank. He had a small face, a little beak, and a bulbous head. He was the smallest of whales at fifteen feet in length and three thousand pounds—rather like a large dolphin with a basketball head.

"Tell me about Veero," Glenna requested of Chloe.

The young mother-to-be absently patted her round stomach as she stared at the white whale. "We think Veero is about fifteen years old. He was trapped by fishermen in the Arctic and was injured. We're thankful they were more interested in rescuing him than killing him, and sent him to a research center in Greenland. He's been moved three times before coming here because no one had the facilities to care for him long term. This was five years ago."

"He was separated from his pod by the fishermen?" Glenna asked. She knew belugas usually swam in groups of ten whales or more.

"That's the funny thing. Veero was alone. We think he may have been separated through an attack by orcas. It's difficult to say. He didn't bear any scars from an attack, but he behaved as though he'd been severely injured. It took many months of intensive care to get him back into good condition. There's no plan to reintroduce him into the wild. Many people who've studied him believe he would die within months of the reintroduction."

Glenna watched Gary drop fish into the tank. Her dad held the bucket of fish. Glenna was sure her dad was plying Gary with questions about the whale. He loved marine life more than anything. A wide grin spread across his face as he watched Veero scoop the snack into his mouth and swallow the fish whole. He wasn't in his wheelchair, insisting he felt strong enough today without it. Glenna reluctantly agreed. She had to remember that God had promised to watch over her dad. Otherwise he would have reminded her not to parent him.

Chloe touched Glenna's arm. "I'm so glad your father was up to the trip, Glenna. I've wanted to make his acquaintance but never had the chance. He's a legend in his field."

Chloe had probably never met him because he'd been in prison. Glenna still couldn't understand how such a brilliant man could make stupid mistakes over and over. What made a man with so much potential want to steal from others? It made no sense. Yet she had to remind herself he was a changed man because of the Lord.

Brent joined the men on the platform. He wore a black wetsuit that covered him from head to ankles. Glenna watched as he slipped into the water with the white whale. Veero let out a piercing whistle and several short squeals, then charged toward Brent.

Glenna's stomach clenched with fear as she watched Brent kicking in the water. The whale would be upon him in less than a second. "Is it okay for him to be in there with the whale?" she gasped.

"Oh, sure!" Chloe laughed. "Brent and Veero are old friends. The only problem is, the water's so cold because Veero is from the Arctic. He has a thick layer of blubber to keep him comfortable, but Brent has only the wetsuit. He won't be able to stay in there long, but I'm sure they'll make the most of the time."

Glenna watched in fascination as Brent ran his hand along the back of the whale. Veero tossed his head and chirped happily. When Brent dove under the water suddenly, the whale mimicked him. They surfaced together, and Glenna thought the whale would be smiling if he could. Brent certainly was.

"Tell me about Brent," Glenna said suddenly, turning to Chloe. "You've known him a long time."

Glenna tried to hide her curiosity from Chloe's watchful gaze. She knew she wasn't fooling her though.

"Do you care for him?"

"He's one of my employees," Glenna answered casually. "I just want to know more."

Chloe turned her attention back to Brent and the whale, and Glenna thought she wasn't going to get an answer. Chloe rested her hands on her tummy, and a slight smile curved her lips.

"Of all the people I know, Brent has changed the most. For instance, the last time he was with Veero he did a cannonball into the water to show off for some girls. Today he slipped into the water to satisfy himself and no one else. He's always had a good heart, just mixed-up priorities. Now, because of God, those priorities are straightened out. That's all I can tell you, Glenna. The rest you'll have to ask Brent himself."

Glenna stifled a sigh of frustration. She already knew these things about Brent, and they didn't answer her deepest questions or assuage her unending doubts. What had he done to land in prison? She knew all she had to do was ask and he would tell her everything she wanted to know; yet she was afraid to hear the truth. Would knowing the truth change how she felt about him? She couldn't deny that she was beginning to care deeply for him despite her best efforts to ignore those feelings. He was kind and gentle and reliable. But what if he was too good to be true and the bottom dropped out of his ideal character? In her experience, ex-cons weren't as perfect as Brent, regardless of how much they'd changed.

Prison cells don't have to have bars. They come in the form of marriage to an inmate. Her mother's words came unbidden from the past. She could see her mother's look of misery when her father called from the police station that last time—so hopeless and angry. Was it worth it to risk repeating the past? If she allowed herself to love Brent, she would inevitably create a world of disappointment and pain for them both.

Don't let your past determine your future.

The thought was so strong that Glenna thought it came as an audible voice. She turned to Chloe, but her friend's attention was focused on Gary. The words hadn't been part of her mother's admonishments from the past. These words pointed her in a different direction.

Was that what she did—allow her past to determine her future? Yes, she admitted to herself, she did, and she couldn't help it. Her mother's warnings were so strong, and she didn't want to repeat her mother's mistakes.

"Hey, Glenna!" Gary came up behind her, catching her unawares. Chloe smiled when he wrapped his arms around both women's shoulders. His hands smelled of fish, and both Glenna and Chloe grimaced and shoved him away. Chloe started giggling when he sputtered in protest.

"All right, all right! I'll go wash my hands! Then we need to do the necessary paperwork so Glenna can ship Brent's playmate to New York."

Glenna spent the rest of the afternoon watching Veero and arranging for his transfer, but her thoughts were continually on Brent and the answers Chloe refused to disclose.

After a busy day Glenna's father told her he'd rather turn in early at the hotel than go out to dinner. Talking with Gary about recent changes in the industry plus spending time with Veero had worn him out. Since his stroke he fatigued more easily than he used to. Glenna knew he'd spent too much time on his feet, but she wouldn't scold him. He'd had so much fun that she couldn't fault him. But tonight she wished he could muster a little more energy for her sake; she wasn't sure she wanted to be alone with Brent. It felt too much like a date, and it made her nervous. She wanted to be with Brent and get to know him better; yet she was afraid to learn too much. When it came to Brent Parker, Glenna found it increasingly more difficult to keep her heart separated from other matters.

Brent made Glenna feel even more confused when he picked her up at her room. She'd prepared herself to receive him cordially as a friend. There wasn't anything between them so she shouldn't be nervous. Yet one glance at him made butterflies tumble in her stomach. He looked exceedingly handsome in crisp khaki slacks and a navy button-down shirt. She was used to seeing him in faded T-shirts and cut-off denim shorts. It was hard to treat him like an employee when she kept forgetting she was the boss. No wonder most companies frowned on dating in the workplace. Yet Glenna knew this was an unusual situation, and the mammal sanctuary was no typical company. If anything, all the unwritten rules for businesses had been broken years ago when her father took over the sanctuary from her grandfather.

Glenna was glad she'd chosen a simple red sundress that made her feel feminine and attractive. By the appreciative look in Brent's green eyes, she guessed he approved. She nervously picked at the folds of the dress, trying to think of something witty to say. What was wrong with her? She'd never tried to impress a man. Why start now?

"Hungry?" Brent asked.

Glenna nodded, forcing a smile to her lips. If it weren't for the knot in her stomach, she'd be starved. How did she ever think she could just be friends with this man? On the other hand, how could she allow anything else?

"If we keep standing here, Glenna, my stomach is going to declare war against my mouth for not feeding it."

Glenna grinned at the silly mental picture. His words broke through her nervous reaction and melted her tension. She linked her arm through his and tugged him away from the door. "Let's not keep your stomach waiting!"

They walked the short distance to the restaurant, neither making an effort at conversation. Both had slipped into a comfortable mood. Glenna didn't feel nervous anymore; neither did she feel like chatting. She wasn't good at small talk anyway, and Brent didn't seem to mind her silence. It was a beautiful evening—warm and pleasant. She didn't want to ruin it with idle conversation.

With a protective hand at the small of her back, Brent guided her into the restaurant. It was a small, dimly lit bistro and much more intimate than Glenna had expected. All the anxious knots came back. This was a real date. She swallowed nervously as they were seated in a secluded corner, then picked up her menu.

"You're hiding from me, Glenna. Why?" Brent asked as he peered at her over the top of the menu, tipping it down with his index finger. His eyes flashed at her, and he gave her an enigmatic smile. "If you hide, I can't admire you."

The compliment warmed Glenna from her toes up, but she wasn't about to let him know that. "You shouldn't say such things to me, Brent. We have to work together." She had to keep this light and professional, she reminded herself. But who was she kidding? She was more confused now than ever.

"Can't I compliment you? I care about you, and I think you like me, as well. Am I right, Glenna, or is my imagination getting carried away?"

Glenna wanted to tell him it was in his head, but she knew it would be a lie. Ever since he carried her in his arms from the beach to tend her injured foot she'd felt differently toward him. She wasn't ready to put those feelings into words, though. "There's something between us. You're not imagining anything," she murmured. Color crept into her cheeks as a slow grin of satisfaction spread across his face. She was saved from further comment when the waiter came and took their order.

Soon their food arrived, and Glenna was careful to steer the conversation to neutral topics. She felt herself relaxing as the evening wore on. Brent made her laugh at his stories until tears filled her eyes. He teased her and provoked her. When she playfully lashed back it was obvious she delighted him by the way his eyes twinkled as he chuckled. This was how he treated Crystal, she realized, and she liked it. She found herself enjoying Brent's company in a way she never had with a man.

As the conversation lulled, a shadow crossed Glenna's thoughts. Chloe Erickson had said if there was anything more she wanted to know, she had to ask Brent. Glenna took a deep breath, trying to justify her curiosity.

"Brent, may I ask you something?" she asked seriously. Her tone drew a puzzled frown from him. When his intent gaze met hers, she swallowed around the lump in her throat. It shouldn't be so hard to ask why a person had been committed to prison.

"What do you want to know, Glenna?"

She dropped her gaze, wishing she hadn't started this, but she couldn't turn back. The question had bothered her since he walked into her office for an interview. She could have dug up the information herself, but something always prevented her. Even her father knew the details, but she'd been left in the dark. It only seemed right for her to know the truth, and yet she hesitated.

"Just ask. Anything you want to know, I'll tell you," he encouraged gently.

Glenna straightened in her seat and stared across the table at him. "All right." She took a deep breath. "Tell me why you went to prison."

She expected him to freeze up or react with cynicism, anything but the sigh of—satisfaction? He was actually smiling.

"I took some eggs," he answered calmly.

Had she heard him correctly? "Eggs."

Brent nodded solemnly. "Not just any eggs. They were endangered Kemp's ridley turtle eggs. Highly valued and protected. Poachers contacted me with an offer I couldn't refuse at the time because I was broke and stupid. I stole the eggs Gary was supposed to take back to the States for observation. People in Mexico use those eggs, believing they serve all sorts of medicinal purposes. I was only too happy to make a few bucks off their superstitions. I was pretty desperate for the cash back then."

This wasn't what Glenna had expected to hear. She didn't know what she'd anticipated, but stealing turtle eggs hadn't been it. She sagged back in her chair with relief.

"I won't steal turtle eggs from you, Glenna. You have my word on that."

"But I don't have any turtle eggs."

Brent shook his head, staring at her in all seriousness. "That's not what I mean. I'm trying to tell you that you can trust me. I made a mistake and paid the price for it. But more than that, I've had a change of heart. I'm never going back."

"You don't have to tell me this, Brent. I don't need any assurances." As she said the words she realized how true they were. She trusted Brent. But, she wondered, could he trust her?

❧

As they left the restaurant to walk back to their hotel rooms, a chilly breeze rose in the air. Brent wanted the night to last forever. Glenna seemed to enjoy his company, and he didn't remember when he'd felt so comfortable with a woman. She could be bristly on the outside; yet on the inside she was gentle and even vulnerable.

She was his other half.

He knew it in his heart as though God had placed the confirmation within him. Glenna was the woman he wanted to spend the rest of his life with. Tonight was a good beginning. She'd allowed him to draw within those walls she had erected around her heart, and he was able to glimpse the tenderness he knew was hidden there. She amazed him. She was small yet so capable, taking on responsibilities stronger people would balk at. Yet she never complained. She accepted her tasks willingly. And he admired her for it. No, admire wasn't the right word; he loved her for it. If only he could convince her she could share those responsibilities without sacrificing any integrity—and share them with him.

He'd waited weeks for her to ask him about his time in prison. He hadn't wanted to volunteer the information. She had been curious, no doubt, but she never got close enough to question him. Finally she'd asked. It had been so liberating to lay the truth on the table for her inspection. And her relief had been evident. Stealing turtle eggs was a serious offense but obviously not what Glenna had expected. Whatever her suspicions or fears, he was glad to have laid them to rest.

When Glenna shivered, rubbing her arms briskly, Brent was more than happy to lend her his warmth. She didn't seem to mind when he draped his arm around her shoulders and tucked her close to his side. "Is that better?"

Briefly she nodded and looked up at him with shining eyes that made his heart quicken. How he'd dreamed she would look at him like that! He needed to tell her he'd fallen in love with her.

Brent was absorbed in trying to find the right words to tell Glenna how he felt. He slowed his steps, reluctant to part with her until she knew what was in his heart. Behind them a dark figure stepped out of an alley and followed them along the quiet street. "Glenna, I need to tell you something." He slowed his steps even more. She turned, looking up at him expectantly.

"I know you feel cautious about me, and it's understandable because of what you've been through. We've become friends, and I'd like to be more. I want you to know that I—"

"Hey, my brother, Brent!" someone called out of the darkness.

Brent stiffened at the greeting but didn't turn. It was a voice out of his worst nightmare—a haunting voice from the past. He'd never expected to hear that sound, and a sudden panic gripped him. They had to get out of there fast! "Come on, Glenna. Let's go! Now!"

Glenna hastened her steps to match his. No one else was on the street, and Brent wished he hadn't chosen such a secluded restaurant. It had been stupid of him. He did not want to get caught alone without a way to defend himself and Glenna.

"Come on, Parker! Wait up!" Footsteps pounded on the concrete behind them.

"You got a hearing problem, buddy?"

Brent was jerked to a stop when a man's strong hand grabbed his hair. He winced with the sharp pain, then froze when he heard the snap of a switchblade opening. Hearing Glenna's gasp made him cringe even more. He'd do anything to spare her such a scene, but he could only pray God would deliver them safely.

Slowly Brent turned to face his aggressor, keeping Glenna tucked closely behind him. He wasn't surprised to see the men who had caused him so much trouble a few years earlier. They hadn't been responsible for putting him in prison, but they'd drawn him into many dangerous activities. Brent had hoped he would never see them again.

The leader of the three men was shorter than Brent but made up for his lack of height with meanness. The other two were big, dumb, and dangerous.

"We been looking for you a long time, Parker. You go on a long vacation?"

"Something like that." Brent stood his ground, eyeing the leader boldly. This man no longer had any hold on him.

"It's nice you showed up. See, we have a little job for you." He fingered the thin moustache that covered his upper lip as his eyes narrowed on Brent's closed expression. "You got a problem with this?"

Brent didn't move his gaze from the leader. "Yeah, I have a problem with it."

He'd known these guys when he was in college. They were notorious drug dealers. Brent had never been involved with their illegal activities, even when he'd been desperate for cash. His only slip-up had been stealing the turtle eggs. Now he was intent on keeping his freedom. Since Christ had set him apart, he'd entered the Father's rest. Nothing would make him hook up with these guys again. "I'm not doing you any favors, Ruben."

"Who said anything about a favor? You're going to do this for me because I said, or you might have to feel a little pain first. And then you'll do it." Ruben sneered as he snapped his fingers. Before Brent knew what was happening, one of the thugs stepped forward with a swift jab to Brent's midsection.

"Stop it!" Glenna screamed as Brent doubled over in pain. "Leave him alone!"

Ruben turned to Glenna with new interest. "Who do we have here? Are you Parker's little friend?" he asked with false friendliness. "Maybe you could help him make up his mind. He always was stubborn and didn't respond well to pain. But if you were in pain—"

Brent rushed at Ruben. No one was going to hurt Glenna. Before he could reach the arrogant thug he was met with a hard hook to his chin that left him spinning. While he regained his bearings one of the guys grabbed Glenna.

"Don't touch me, or you'll be sorry," she warned.

The men laughed. Brent didn't know what she was going to do, but he knew not to underestimate Glenna.

When the man holding Glenna tightened his grip, she started screaming and didn't stop long enough to take a breath. Her shrill shrieking filled the quiet street and drew attention from the few businesses that were still open. People came to the doors to stare, but no one ventured forth.

"Help me! Call the police! These men are attacking me!"

Her display distracted the punks long enough for Brent to break away and shove the man who held Glenna. The man fell backward, and Brent grabbed Glenna and started running. They raced back the way they had come, back toward the restaurant. Unfortunately they didn't make it far before their pursuers caught up with them.

Brent knew they were in bigger trouble than before because Ruben would be angry. Anyone who valued his well-being didn't upset Ruben.

"We're finished messing around, Parker," Ruben hissed. His black eyes flashed at Brent. He stroked the cobra tattooed to the back of his fist, then flexed his fingers. Brent guessed he was about to feel the violence of the man's temper. *Dear God, don't let them beat me up in front of Glenna. She doesn't need to be a part of this!*

In the distance a police siren sounded.

Ruben lowered his fist and shoved Brent toward the darkened alley. "Lock them in the warehouse. We don't have time to deal with this now. We'll come back when the cops are gone."

Brent and Glenna were herded into the alley and through a metal door in the side of the building. A sliver of light filtered in from a broken window high above the door.

"We'll be back to deal with you, Parker," Ruben threatened.

"Let Glenna go, Ruben. She has nothing to do with this."

Ruben laughed. It was a hollow sound that echoed around the empty room. "She's involved because you're involved. Don't go anywhere!" He snickered as he backed out of the warehouse. Then they heard the sound of a metal bolt sliding into place.

Brent strained to hear the men return, but all was silent in the alley. He groped his way to the door and struggled in vain to open it. The door was held from the outside, and Brent could do nothing to force it open. They were trapped until Ruben and his cronies decided to return and finish what they started.

"Brent, where are you?" Glenna cried out, her voice tight.

He could hear her fumbling in the darkness. He made his

way to her and folded her in his arms. She was doubtless trying to maintain control but still might be close to collapsing after the strain. It was his fault. He never should have returned to Galveston. It was ridiculous to think he could walk around his old haunts and not be recognized. Now Glenna was involved, and he'd give anything to see her set free.

"It's okay. We're going to be fine."

His shirt felt wet where Glenna pressed her face, and Brent's heart sank. She didn't shudder or make any sound, but her tears blazed a path straight to his heart. He tightened his arms around her, searching for the right words to say. No apology seemed adequate for what he'd done to her.

"Brent, how could you?" came her muffled question.

He stiffened, knowing he deserved her accusations. She'd never forgive him after this. "I know—"

"How could you stand there and not fight back?" She looked up at him with her tear-stained cheeks. He couldn't make out her face in the darkness; yet it was easy for him to reach out and wipe away her tears. He knew her face by heart. "I wanted to hurt them when they hit you. I've never felt that way in my life," she whispered.

"I know, sweetheart." The endearment slipped easily from his lips. "But striking back wouldn't have done any good. It would have made matters worse, and I wanted to spare you that scene. I wish you hadn't seen any of it. You deserve better. I wanted so much to impress you and make you like me more. Instead I showed you the gutter I used to live in."

"But you don't live there anymore. You're far above this."

He hugged her close, grateful for her acceptance.

"Brent, I—"

Any further words were silenced in the darkness as he bent his head and kissed her. After a moment he pulled away slightly. "I hope you don't mind. I guess I should have asked you first."

"I wanted you to. That's what I was going to ask. But I didn't know how and wasn't sure it was right anyway. I mean, I can't make any promises about the future."

"I thought you might need to be comforted, and that was the best way I knew how then." Brent pulled her close again. "This has been a terrible end to our perfect night."

He would do anything to take away the fear and uncertainty she felt, rather than add to it. If the kiss helped, he would be glad. She might wake up tomorrow and hate him for putting her through this terrible experience. And when Ruben returned, the night would only get worse. But Brent didn't want to think about the moment when the door swung open and he would face Ruben again.

"Brent, we have to pray—now." Glenna broke away from his embrace. "We're stuck in this warehouse, and it's too dark to find another way out. We don't know when those horrible men are going to return. Let's pray while we still have the chance, before they come back and—" Her words stopped. He could only imagine she was thinking about what they would do to them.

At once Brent knelt, unmindful of the floor beneath him. He was surprised when Glenna followed him. She slipped her fingers into his hand, and together they prayed.

"Father, forgive me for getting us into this terrible situation. Lord, You know I never wanted to be involved with these men in the first place, and I pray You will rescue us from them tonight. We can't escape without Your help, and we're afraid. Yet I know You promise to protect us. Please, Lord, get us out of here. Thank You for Glenna and her strength. Please comfort her as only You can. Thank You, Father, for

Your mercy and Your creativity. And we put our trust in You. Amen."

As Glenna murmured her own "amen," they heard the sound of the bolt sliding back against the metal door. Ruben had returned! Brent's heart started pounding in his chest. He scrambled to his feet and helped Glenna to hers.

Whatever happened next, his fate was in God's capable hands.

The door swung open with a scraping squawk and banged against the wall. A bright light shone in Brent's eyes. He reached up to shield himself from the glare, not expecting the intense light. Something wasn't right.

"Looks like we've found the rest of the gang. You! Put your hands up where I can see them!"

It was the police! Brent raised his hands as he sagged inwardly with relief. Ruben wouldn't be back to finish the job. His relief vanished when the officer stepped forward and slapped handcuffs on his wrists.

"What are you doing?" Glenna exclaimed. "He has nothing to do with those guys!" She stepped between the officer and Brent. "Arrest that gang of idiots, but leave Brent alone!"

eight

You have the wrong guy!" Glenna protested again when the officers ignored her. She couldn't believe they would arrest Brent without asking any questions first. This was still a free country.

"We have reason to believe this man is involved with a gang of drug dealers," one of the officers patiently explained, as though she were a dim-witted two-year-old.

"And I say your reasons are wrong! This man works for me in Long Beach, New York, and we're in the area on a business trip. As we were walking down the street your gang of drug dealers attacked us. The only way he's involved is by trying to defend us from those guys!"

The officer paused and threw his partner a look of uncertainty. Glenna prayed the police would listen to sound reason and leave Brent alone. He wasn't in the wrong any more than she was. Justice had to prevail.

"You don't have any current dealings with the gang in question?" one of the officers asked Brent.

Brent shook his head. "None. I knew them a few years back, but I was never involved in their dealings."

Glenna knew Brent was telling the truth. He couldn't lie and get away with it. She was well versed in detecting falsehoods, having been around enough convicts in her life to read them.

"If you'll just listen to me! We're the victims here—"

Brent's strong fingers slipped over Glenna's shoulder and

gave her a sharp squeeze. "I appreciate this, but I don't need you to defend me, Glenna," he said softly yet firmly.

At his warning Glenna clamped her mouth shut. She was so accustomed to taking care of everyone that it never occurred to her *not* to take care of Brent.

Brent straightened and looked the officer right in the eye. "I haven't been in the area for a few years, but I'm willing to give you any information I can."

"I'm sure we can discuss this down at the station," the officer said as he jerked at the cuffs on Brent's wrists.

Glenna was appalled. This wasn't how it was supposed to work. "But you can't take him—"

Brent gave her a warning look and shook his head, silencing any further arguments she might have. "Go back to the hotel and your dad. I'll be along shortly," he promised. Glenna hoped he was right and that she wouldn't have to post bail.

❧

Two hours passed while Glenna wore a path in the carpet in her hotel room. She didn't dare go to her dad and tell him Brent had been arrested. Brent was different from the con men she'd known—he was guilty of stealing eggs, not holding up Fort Knox. He was innocent now, but she didn't want to explain this to her dad. It was too complicated and ridiculous. She hoped Brent would show up before breakfast and save her from the questions that would arise from his absence.

At a quarter to ten a soft rap sounded at the door of her room. Glenna rushed to look through the peephole. Brent stood, waiting patiently on the other side. Glenna unbolted the door and threw herself into his arms.

"Everything is okay, Glenna. I promise," Brent assured her as his arms tightened around her. He stroked her back with small, soothing circles. "You have nothing to worry about."

"I was so worried. I hated every minute of it." She wondered suddenly if this was how her mother felt every time her father was arrested. It was no wonder she had warned her daughter to stay away from men with prison sentences. But Brent was different from her father. He was innocent, and that caused Glenna to worry about him even more. She held him tightly, ignoring the tears of relief that sprang to her eyes. She was scared for him and angry—and so relieved he was back. The fact that she felt safer in his arms than anywhere else made no sense. She should be running scared from the threat he posed to her peace of mind rather than snuggling closer in his arms. "I prayed for you, but I didn't know what was happening or if you'd be released tonight. I didn't know what to do."

"You did the right thing, Glenna. Everything is all right. They didn't actually arrest me. Ruben and his gang are in custody, and the charges should put them away for a while. I'd like to leave this behind us and forget it ever happened."

"I'd like that, too," she murmured. She didn't resist when his lips lowered over hers. He paused as though allowing her a chance to pull away. When she didn't protest, he took possession of her lips with a kiss that melted away the fear and worry that had held her captive all evening.

❧

Veero settled into his new home quickly and brought an incredible amount of interest to the sanctuary. People from all over the state flocked to see the new white whale. Students from the elementary level up to post-graduate came to study him. Veero loved the attention, squealing and chirping at all the right times. It seemed another of Brent's ideas was working its magic, bringing the sanctuary into a state of financial success as private donations poured in. Yet Brent gave all the glory to God, never accepting a word of recognition. Glenna didn't know how she got along before he came to work for her.

Brent took over the responsibility for the whale, and Glenna was happy to leave him to it. He had become so engrossed in promoting and caring for the new "star" that he gave Glenna little attention. She had a feeling, however, that he was intentionally giving her space to sort out her own feelings. Neither mentioned the kisses they had shared in Galveston, and Glenna was relieved. How could she explain to him that she now realized it had been a mistake? She had her reasons for feeling that way, but she wasn't sure she could make Brent understand. If he'd tried to pursue the topic, she would have explained it to him, but he never said a word.

"A con man will break your heart, Glenna, and while he's doing time, you'll be picking up the pieces." Her mother's words echoed in her mind as a warning from the past. She was afraid to follow her mother's footsteps. Her family had made enough mistakes. It was her job to turn that record around. Falling in love with a man who had spent time in prison was not a step in the right direction. Her father had caused so much pain with his choices, and her mother devastated her family when she left. Glenna couldn't let it happen in her own life. It was a good thing this particular ex-con was too busy to pay her any mind.

Keith Dempsen, on the other hand, had plenty of time to devote to Glenna. The more successful the sanctuary became, the more anxious Keith seemed. Glenna didn't want to deal with him or his business offers any longer, but the distraction he provided kept her thoughts off Brent. She knew Brent was waiting for her to make the next move. All he needed was a little encouragement to begin drawing her into a closer relationship. What scared her was how she longed for him to do that. He said little during the day, but she was aware that his gaze followed her every move. He was waiting.

Keith wasn't.

⁊⋅

Glenna was busy reviewing the new commercial for the mammal sanctuary when the phone rang in her office. Absently she answered it, never taking her gaze from the television screen. It had been Brent's idea to promote Veero through all available media. The first commercial had tripled donations.

"Marine Mammal Sanctuary—may I help you?"

"Say you'll go out to dinner with me tonight, and that will be the greatest help of all."

Glenna stiffened at the sound of Keith's voice. "I thought you were out of town for a few days," she said, disappointed her respite was over. He had flown to Charleston two days earlier for an emergency meeting, probably to discuss her reluctance to sell. She'd hardly noticed his absence because she was so busy with the sanctuary, but now she realized it had been a relief to have him gone.

"A corporate jet makes business trips pass more quickly. What's your answer about dinner? It's urgent I meet with you. It would have been much simpler if you had accompanied me on my trip. It would have solved many problems. But for now, let's talk dinner. What do you say?"

Glenna hesitated, not liking the pressure he was laying on so thick. "Excuse me?"

"Dinner. I asked you to dinner."

"I don't think so, Keith. I have things to do, and you sound rushed, too."

"I'm not rushed. I'm just feeling a little pressure because

the screws are tightening. But let's not talk shop. I have something entirely different I want to discuss with you tonight. So you have to join me for dinner."

Glenna knew it was time to set things straight with Keith. She'd allowed him to manipulate her and back her into a corner for far too long. She had done her best to stand up to his coercion. It was difficult to fight a corporation and its smooth executive, even with the limited legal aid she received from the county. The prayers of her family and everyone at church had made a significant difference in her finances, and God had answered with abundance. Now with the sanctuary's new success she could afford a lawyer, briefly, to help her stand against Delta Ray's assault. She knew she couldn't afford a lengthy battle, but maybe she'd be able to convince Keith to back off. Either way she planned to tell him there would be no more business dinners and if he needed to contact her, he could do so through the mail.

"All right. I can spare a little time this evening," she agreed cautiously, fully expecting him to make another play for the property. "I have a few things I need to say, too."

As soon as they sat down at the restaurant, Glenna informed Keith of the changes she planned. He didn't balk when she said no more dinner meetings. He didn't scoff when she said she would hire a lawyer to support her stand against Delta Ray Investments. And he didn't even blink when she said she didn't want any more contact with him. This puzzled her. She'd expected him to bluster or criticize her. It almost seemed he didn't hear her.

As they ate, Glenna was left to wonder what Keith wanted to discuss with her. He purposely steered the conversation away from anything remotely personal—or professional for that matter. He didn't talk about the property, which was surprising because he usually discussed that first. She watched him fidget with his silverware as he talked about everything from the weather to politics; yet never did he broach the serious topic he said he'd needed to discuss with her. He seemed nervous as he studiously avoided her pointed gazes.

When he started to talk about next week's weather forecast, Glenna had had enough. "What's wrong? Either tell me what's going on or take me home."

Dark color crept up his neck as Keith grimaced. "You're right. I've been trying all night to do this, and I need to be direct. You're a no-nonsense woman, so of course the direct approach is best."

Glenna frowned. She tried to follow his thinking, but so far she felt lost at sea without a preserver. Keith wasn't acting like himself.

Keith straightened and reached into his breast pocket, pulling out a tiny object. He opened his fist so Glenna could see what he held. On his palm was a gold ring with an enormous diamond solitaire. Glenna stared at him in shock. He stared back at her, looking like a desperate little boy.

"Marry me. We've talked about this before, I know. But you never gave me an answer."

"I just told you I won't see you anymore—professionally or otherwise!"

When he reached for her hand, Glenna snatched it away, pressing her fist to her breast. She couldn't begin to describe the surprise and dismay his proposal caused. But words weren't necessary—Keith could read her reaction in her eyes.

"I know this seems a little sudden. But—"

"But nothing! You and I don't share the same faith. We have nothing in common, and we're complete strangers."

"That's not true. I've known you for nearly a year," Keith

stated—which she couldn't refute—as he ignored her protest over their unequal faiths. She'd known Brent for even less time, but if he had been the one—

"I'm not your type. I have a strong faith in God, and He's at the center of my life. We really have nothing to discuss," Glenna argued, wondering what she would have said if Brent had been the one to propose. He did share her faith and many of the same interests. They were friends now. She would have been tempted to accept his proposal, but she knew that would have meant disaster for both of them. She needed to tell Brent why it was impossible for them to be more than friends, but first she had to deal with Keith.

"Don't you think I know my own mind? I can decide who my type is, Glenna, and I've chosen you. Don't you want me? Can't you even consider it?" He didn't give her a chance to answer before continuing, "I'm not doing this just for us. I'm thinking of your father, as well. He's not in the best of health. Wouldn't you want him to feel secure, knowing his daughter is taken care of? As it is, you have to work so hard, and it must bother him a great deal."

If he was appealing to her sense of guilt, he was doing a good job. Of course she hated the worry her dad shouldered along with the condemnation he felt over his condition. He wanted to help with the sanctuary, but he wasn't physically able. She was so afraid he felt trapped in a new kind of prison—one where he wasn't allowed to do anything because of his health, not because of confinement. Keith had hit on a sore subject, and he knew it.

"I'm not trying to make you feel bad, Glenna. I simply want you to consider everything before you decide. Our marriage would make life better for your family. But I don't want you to agree because of them. I want you to accept me because you want me. We could be good for each other."

Glenna stared at him in stony silence, trying to think of the right words to answer him. She had no question in her mind that they would be wrong for each other. This was just another manipulation. He was using her sense of guilt to sway her, but she wouldn't be moved. No matter what Keith offered, it wouldn't be enough to get her to turn her back on the truth and her values. She believed in God, hard work, and trustworthiness. Keith had given her nothing but difficulties since the day she met him.

Brent's face came to mind again. He was the other reason she couldn't accept Keith's offer of marriage. She was falling for a man with a prison record. The thought made her uneasy because she knew the possible consequences; yet her feelings wouldn't be denied. Brent had found a way to touch her heart even when she did everything to prevent it from happening.

When she stood to leave, Keith gripped her hand. "Don't go. I want you to take the ring. Think about it. You don't have to answer tonight."

"I've already answered, Keith. I won't marry you."

"I won't accept that answer." He pried open her fingers and placed the ring on her palm before closing her fingers around it. "At least think about it. Please, Glenna." He squeezed her hand, and the diamond bit into her palm. With some effort, she forced herself to nod.

"I've actually thought about this quite a lot, Keith. My answer won't change, so you can take your ring back."

Keith pulled his hands away. "And I don't have a box for it. It suits you, Glenna. Wear it tonight. Take it home and think about it. That's all I'm asking. Remember the gold bracelet with the tiny dolphins? You wouldn't take that either. At least do this, please?"

Glenna realized people were staring at them and she was making a scene. Reluctantly she sat back in her seat, laying the ring on the table between them. She wouldn't take it, nor would she allow him to coerce her into accepting it.

Keith finally reached for the ring and slipped it back into his pocket, a deep scowl on his face.

With nothing more to say they left the restaurant once the bill was paid. The ride back was quiet. She knew her reaction had angered Keith. He seemed different, even vulnerable. Yet an actor could make his audience believe anything.

Keith drove in silence, and Glenna didn't bother attempting conversation. She hoped this would be the last encounter she had with him. If her mother were here, she'd be thrilled with Keith and encourage Glenna to accept him. But she wasn't like her mother, and she couldn't muster any enthusiasm for a man who didn't share her faith. Even their so-called friendship was a farce.

＊

Brent had just slipped behind the wheel of his old battered pickup. It was time to go to his second job, hauling fish for Woody Sewler. It was backbreaking work, but every time a new load of feed fish arrived at the sanctuary, he knew the labor was worth it. With the new success of the mammal sanctuary and Veero's popularity, he hoped he could approach Glenna soon about renegotiating the feed fish issue. She'd have to pay more than she used to, thanks to Keith Dempsen's meddling, but maybe Brent could quit the night job. She needed him at the sanctuary, and he realized the potential there was untapped.

He was about to shove his key in the ignition when Keith's sleek sports car rolled into the parking lot. The car's engine purred like a fine-tuned machine, and Brent was again reminded of the many differences between him and Keith. If he started the pickup right now, the thundering of the tortured engine would wake up half of Long Island. It was an example of the shambles he felt his life was in compared to that of Keith Dempsen, the corporate genius. Keith had money, connections, ambition. What did he, Brent, have to offer Glenna? He had just as much ambition, but his past limited his options. In fact, he was so limited that Glenna shouldn't think twice about him.

"But I have Christ, and no worldly riches can compare with the wealth of what's in my heart," Brent reminded himself. He knew when it came to a comparison between his integrity and what Keith valued, there would be no contest. Keith had already proven he was lacking where it mattered most.

He watched Glenna climb out of the low-slung car. Even in the dimly lit parking lot she looked beautiful in Brent's eyes, like a precious painting to admire for hours at a time. Unfortunately he wasn't her only admirer. Keith also pulled himself from the car and circled around to Glenna's side. Brent had to grip the steering wheel to keep himself from intervening when Keith pulled Glenna into his arms. When Keith tried to kiss her, Brent reached for the door handle.

"No, Keith!" Glenna's voice carried clearly through the night air. She ducked away from Keith's amorous advances but wasn't fast enough. He held her by the neck and pulled her closer so she couldn't avoid his kiss. As she struggled against Keith, Brent's feet hit the pavement.

"They conspire, they lurk, they watch my steps, eager to take my life."

The verse from Psalms caused Brent to slow his steps. He didn't want to do something stupid to land himself back in prison. Then Keith wouldn't have anything standing between him and his pursuit of Glenna. Cautiously he approached them, sticking to the shadows. Soon he was within hearing of every murmur.

"This is what engaged couples are supposed to do, baby," Keith crooned.

Brent stiffened. *Engaged?*

Glenna heaved a mighty shove against Keith's chest. He loosened his grasp as she continued to struggle against him. "We're not engaged, Keith!"

"You're right. I'm sorry." Keith cupped Glenna's cheek as Brent watched the scene like a wary panther. If Keith made one wrong move, Brent was ready to pounce.

"I'll say good night then, Glenna. Please remember what we talked about. I'm anxiously awaiting your answer." This time his romantic overture lacked force as he placed a chaste kiss to her forehead.

"I already gave you my answer," Glenna answered, but Keith didn't seem to hear.

Brent sank lower in the shadows. Glenna, shaking her head, turned and went inside, her heels tapping loudly on the ground as she moved away through the darkness. Brent waited for Keith to slip back into his car and drive away. Instead he stood there and flipped out his cellular phone, then punched in a phone number.

"Dempsen here. Yeah, I did it. No—it was tonight. Did she faint with gratitude? No!" Keith gave a forced bark of laughter. "You'll be amazed. She's the first who hasn't fallen at my feet. No, I wouldn't call her gorgeous, though she's definitely a challenge. No, don't worry. I'll win her over. I've got Glenna Mayfield and this shoddy property in my back pocket. Delta Ray Investments will own this little chunk of land before the close of next month. I'll keep you posted."

Keith chuckled with satisfaction as he stuffed the phone back into his pocket. He strode around the car before sliding behind the wheel.

Brent watched through narrowed eyes as Keith roared out of the parking lot. He didn't know what he was going to do, but he had to stop Keith Dempsen. He'd promised to stand up for Glenna Mayfield. She needed his help more than ever and not just with the marine animals. She didn't know what she was up against with Keith Dempsen. Somehow he had to find a way to protect her. With God's help he wouldn't fail her when she needed him the most.

nine

Glenna paused in the doorway of the kitchen to watch Brent cook. A tantalizing aroma had drawn her, but the sight of him at home in her kitchen captivated her. She hadn't expected to see him in her house, fixing a meal. She had come home to talk to her dad, but he was snoozing on the couch in the living room.

"What are you doing?" she asked.

Brent didn't even look up from the egg he was whisking. "If you need me to explain this, then we're all in trouble." A wide grin split his face, and she knew he was teasing. She wished she didn't blush so easily whenever he toyed with her. It wasn't professional. But who was she kidding? She hadn't thought of Brent as an employee for some time.

"I can cook! Do you want me to help?" She strode into the kitchen to stand at his side.

Brent eyed her doubtfully but handed over the bowl. "We're making meatballs for homemade spaghetti. Your dad told me the other day it's his favorite, so I offered to make it for him. Ground beef, Italian sausage, egg, milk, bread crumbs, and a few spices. Think you can handle it? Or should I warn the fire department?"

Glenna ignored his baiting. "Am I smelling the sauce?"

"Yep." Brent lifted the lid from a large pan on the stove. The rich aroma of spaghetti sauce wafted into the room. It smelled spicy and made Glenna's mouth water.

"Where'd you learn to cook?" she asked, as Brent handed her various ingredients.

"Prison. It wasn't as glamorous as this, though. Where'd you learn to cook?"

He didn't elaborate as she'd hoped. It was obvious he didn't want to talk about his past, and suddenly Glenna wasn't so interested in answering questions either. Most little girls learned to cook from mothers and grandmothers. She hadn't.

But he'd answered her question so she owed him the same. "I taught myself. We ate a lot of peanut butter and jelly the first year until I learned how to use the microwave." She could feel Brent's gaze on her face. She knew her every mood reflected there and hated that she couldn't hide anything from him. "Have you noticed Dad won't touch a peanut butter sandwich?" she added, forcing her voice to sound light.

"What about your mom? No one ever mentions Mrs. Mayfield."

Glenna shrugged as a headache suddenly started to form. Thinking about her mom always caused her some type of discomfort. "That's because there isn't anything worth mentioning. How much garlic do you want me to add?"

"Enough to taste but not enough to make everyone pucker." He took the spice bottle from her fingers and measured out a generous amount. "Your mom died when you were little?"

Died? Hardly! How could she explain to Brent that her mother fell in love with a brilliant man who couldn't stay out of prison despite his genius? After bailing him out twelve too many times, Mary Mayfield had had enough. She apologized to her two daughters who were too young to understand her reasons. Then she left, never to be seen again. The worst thing anyone could ever say to her was that she resembled her mother. That was her biggest fear.

"No, she didn't die. Should I add some basil?" She vigorously beat the concoction, wishing Brent would leave the subject alone. Couldn't they cook in peace and leave old bones alone? Brent took the bowl from her hands. Glenna hardly noticed.

She couldn't change what happened to her as a child. Her mother chose to leave her responsibilities, giving them all to Glenna. Only through the grace of God had she held it all together. The last thing she wanted to do was analyze it with Brent.

"There's freedom in forgiveness."

"Did you say something?" She glanced at Brent. He was bent over the meat mixture she'd made a mess of and was stirring the ingredients.

"Nope."

Your mother left, but I was always there for you. You accepted My love. Now accept the freedom I offer.

Glenna wiped her hands on the front of her slacks as she backed toward the doorway. "I—I just remembered there's something I need to do. I should go. Yep, I have to go," she stammered, her eyes wide.

What was happening to her? She didn't want to deal with this—not now! She didn't want to think about her mother and the things she kept bottled within her heart. Her life was okay; she was satisfied. Why did God have to stir up things now?

Brent watched her closely but didn't say anything. He seemed to be wordlessly drawing her toward him so he could comfort her over the losses she experienced as a child. It would have been easy to step into his embrace and accept the compassion that was clearly written in his expression. But Glenna couldn't do it. If she accepted the love of this ex-con, she would ruin his life forever.

❧

It didn't take a genius to know Glenna shouldn't be alone. Brent quickly turned down the burner on the stove so the sauce wouldn't scorch, shoved the meatball mixture into the refrigerator, and followed her. Whether she realized it or not, God had put Glenna into Brent's care, and he wasn't going to fail her now. He loved her, and if it took the rest of his life, he would prove to her how deeply he cared. She might hate his past, but that didn't stop him from loving her. He'd tried to fight it for as long as he could, but it became evident to him that what he felt for Glenna was the real thing. And it wasn't going away.

It didn't take long for Brent to trace Glenna's steps. At first he thought she might have gone back to work, but with all the tourists, she wouldn't have a moment to regain her composure. His second guess proved true. She had gone down to the beach, seeking solitude from curious stares and too many questions. If his intrusion offended her, he'd leave as quickly as he'd come. But he was banking on the fact that she needed someone, even though she was used to fending for herself.

"Why did you follow me?" she questioned as he came near. Her eyes were watery with tears, and her nose was red. Brent reached into his pocket and pulled out his handkerchief.

"Just making sure you're okay. Want to talk about it?"

"No!" she said sharply, then blew her nose.

Brent draped his arm around her waist and pulled her to his side. He was glad she didn't resist. He never doubted his feelings, but he had yet to understand hers. She seemed to trust him though she still hid behind her wall. He wanted to press her to talk, releasing the things she kept locked in her heart. She needed to trust him with those things, too.

"There's more to this than your mom, isn't there? I'm sorry I upset you by asking too many questions." He stopped walking and pulled her in front of him so he could gaze down at her face. The wind whipped at her hair, and she held the curls out of her eyes. A tiny frown puckered her brow as she returned his gaze. "You do too much, you know, Glenna. You take care of everyone in your family, making sure your dad is okay, and you look after Crystal. You've turned the sanctuary into an astounding success. But it's too much for one person. You're going to burn out at this frantic pace." He knew he sounded more like a parent than a friend. "I can help more if you'd let me."

Glenna shook her head. "You already do too much for what you get paid. You're just as much of a workaholic as I am."

"We make a good team." When Glenna stiffened, Brent realized she didn't want to link herself to him.

"Brent, you and I can't be a team. I wish I could make you understand why."

"Try. You can tell me."

Glenna stared up at him for long moments, then sadly shook her head. "I can't."

It hurt, but this wasn't about his feelings. He tried to make his tone sound light. "Anyway, your dad is always telling me what a remarkable job you do. Everyone can see what a success you've made of the place. Even people at church comment on it."

"What about your dad, Brent? You never talk about your family." She studied him curiously with those beautiful blue eyes.

It was only fair to answer her questions if he hoped she would open up to him. He didn't like to talk about his family, because they were so closely connected with the mistakes he'd made. But God had been faithful in forgiving him and turning his life around. He had to trust that God would change his parents' hearts, as well.

"My father is the sheriff in a tiny Texas town. My mother

organizes the social functions for the entire population of five thousand people. They're a little too busy to worry about me."

Brent knew by the frown on Glenna's face that she wasn't satisfied with his answer. He took a deep breath as he drew his gaze away from hers to look toward the ocean. "I was a late-in-life child. My parents had raised two other sons and had two grandchildren when I came along. They were surprised and overwhelmed and had difficulty relating to me from the day I was born. I felt like an only child because my brothers were more than twenty years older than me, and I didn't grow up knowing them well. I tried to please my folks, but they were so involved in their 'adult' life that I often fell by the wayside. I'm not proud to say I rebelled, and that rebellion peaked when I landed myself in prison. When my father, the upstanding sheriff, learned of my shame, he informed me that our relationship would never be the same again. I hurt them with my choices, and they're having a hard time moving past the pain. I've tried to tell them I've turned my life around and am trusting God to help me make wise decisions. They haven't been persuaded yet."

Brent found the telling easier than he'd anticipated. Whether Glenna decided to open up to him didn't matter so much now.

"Do you think that's what I'm doing? That I'm having a hard time moving past the pain, too?"

She looked so lost and forlorn that Brent wanted to take her in his arms and never let her go. But she had to put her trust in God, not in any man's comfort. "How can I answer that when you haven't told me the whole story? You can trust me," Brent responded gently.

Glenna stared up at him as the war raged within her—to tell or to hold her secrets. She opened her mouth; the words were on her lips. Then fear darted into her eyes, and she clamped her mouth shut. Brent had to suppress a groan of frustration as he watched the prize being snatched from his fingertips.

"I can't, Brent. I just can't."

As she hurried up the path to the house, Brent watched her go. She was like a frightened bird seeking the familiarity of her cage. If only she could understand what freedom awaited her on the outside! She couldn't see the riches she held, deposited in her heart by her heavenly Father. Instead she let pain from the past cloud her vision. It was familiar, and she clung to it desperately.

"I'm not giving up, Glenna! And neither should you!" he called. The wind snatched at his words before she could hear them. He hoped he hadn't pushed her too far. If she stopped trusting him, he would have no way of protecting her from Keith. More important, he wouldn't be able to help her find freedom.

❧

Glenna should have taken her conversation with Brent as a forewarning. It never did any good to drag up woes from the past—especially when nothing could be done to set them straight. What was the saying? Let sleeping dogs lie. Now that this beast was resurrected, it had no intention of backing down peacefully.

The day wasn't unusual from most days at the marine sanctuary. The crowds continued to increase, bringing in more money. With satisfaction Glenna had just written out the check for their final debt. She went in search of Brent to see if he wanted to share lunch with her in celebration. He deserved it after all, especially since she had disappointed him. Maybe she could explain that she didn't like to talk about her mother and it was best to leave it alone. God would eventually heal those old hurts if she waited long enough, right?

It was with some shock that she recognized the figure weaving through the crowd ahead of her, moving from one attraction to another—not staying at any of the exhibits long enough to see them.

Glenna gasped, staring at the fair head in horror. "No!"

Her first reaction was to run and hide, but she knew she couldn't do that. It wasn't every day her mother showed up. It was incredible. After ten years of silence, Mary Mayfield had reappeared. Before any of the deeply buried anger and bitterness could swell up, Glenna strode purposefully through the crowd and tapped the familiar person on the shoulder.

The woman turned and stared at Glenna through eyes the same color blue as Crystal's. They were light blue, almost gray, in color. But her gaze was cool and distant, unlike Crystal's. Glenna remembered her mother as a giant; yet now she didn't seem so overwhelming. She seemed frail. Her gaze was fierce and her frown stern, but her body looked weak and weary. Her blond hair wasn't as glossy as Glenna remembered, nor was her skin so rosy. She was pale even under the layers of makeup she wore.

Dear Lord, help me to be strong and say the right things.

Glenna cleared her throat, forcing herself to speak. "Mom. What are you doing here?" She was proud that her voice didn't waver.

"Glenna. Wow. You're all grown up!" Her mom raised her hands to touch Glenna, then let them fall back to her sides.

"Yeah, I guess that happens when ten years go by." An edge of bitterness had crept into her words, which Glenna immediately softened with a forced smile. "Why don't we go to the office and talk? It's quieter, and we won't be disturbed."

Her mother hesitated, and Glenna thought she might refuse, but finally she nodded. "Yes, that's fine. But I only have a few minutes."

A few minutes to spare the daughter she hasn't seen in ten years. Glenna refused to let her thoughts go in that direction. It would only lead to more bitterness.

Together they pushed slowly through the throng of spectators until they reached the administrative office. Glenna opened the door and ushered her mom inside.

Within the small room it was much quieter. They stared at one another in discomfort, searching for something to say—something that would bring them closer after so many years of separation. Was there anything? Glenna searched her mind, but even the mundane didn't form into words. Precious seconds were ticking by, and she couldn't seem to ask the questions she'd had for so long.

"Please make yourself comfortable," Glenna invited, motioning toward a chair. She expected her mom to take a seat across from the desk. Instead she slowly circled the office. Glenna wondered if she was nervous.

"It's incredible," her mother muttered.

"What is?"

Mary Mayfield's laugh was scornful. "I've been gone over a decade, and nothing has changed. Your father was such a slob. Look at all the papers. The mess. The only difference is the computer and fax machine. It's the same secondhand desk that was falling apart years ago. Do you hold it together with tape? And look—the same ugly brown chairs with patches. I'm amazed. Is your father in jail again? Is that why this place is such a mess?"

Of all the imagined reunions, Glenna had never expected one like this. When her mother first left, Glenna dreamed of the day she would return and they would be a family again. Every day she would watch out the window for her mother's arrival. Soon those silly dreams were pushed under her pillow, and she grew up—fast. The last thing her mother had a right to was coming back and ridiculing everything she left behind.

"Dad is at home right now. This *mess*, as you call it, is mine. Why are you here, after all this time?" Glenna suddenly wished she'd never set her gaze on her mother as she walked through the crowded exhibits. Not knowing where she was for all this time was easier to deal with than facing her in person now.

She pretended not to hear the question. Glenna wasn't fooled.

"Who are these people?" her mother asked, picking up a framed snapshot. It was of Glenna, Crystal, and Brent, standing beneath the newly painted front sign.

"That's your other daughter," Glenna answered dryly. She snatched the frame from her mother's hands and put it back on her desk.

"I *know* it's Crystal. Who's the guy?" Keen eyes studied Glenna's face.

"Brent Parker. He's one of the employees." Glenna stared back at her mother. Why were they having this stilted conversation? Wasn't there anything better to talk about, like why she left them and had waited until now to return? Did she really want to hear about Brent? She hadn't asked about their father's health or what Crystal was doing. Her daughters had grown up without her. Didn't she care at all?

"Brent Parker. He's a nice-looking young man."

Glenna blinked, hoping her gaze gave away nothing. She had enough questions in her mind concerning Brent without bringing her mother into the middle. She should have known she would pick up on something.

"You care for him, don't you? This Brent Parker. Just make sure he's nothing like your father." Again she closely watched Glenna's reaction, staring at her with those cool blue eyes.

Glenna reached for a stack of papers, wishing she didn't give her emotions away so easily. What did her mom care if Brent was like her father or not? It wasn't any of her business anymore. She had made certain of that the day she walked out on her family. Glenna fumbled with the papers, averting her gaze. A guilty flush crept up her neck, and she knew her mother wasn't fooled. Glenna had never been able to hide anything from her.

"You're kidding me, Glenna. This man, Brent Parker, is a convict? You've fallen in love with a criminal?"

"No! He's a good, hardworking man. I'd trust him with this business, and I'd trust him with my life. So, yes, in that way he's like Dad. Maybe he spent a little time in prison, but that doesn't matter to me. It shouldn't matter at all. I—I don't know why I'm telling you any of this." Her defense wasn't as strong as she intended, and her mother was quick to take the upper hand.

"Didn't you learn anything from me, Glenna? I told you day in and day out to stay away from men like your father. Didn't you listen to a word I said?"

You've been the voice in my head for as long as I can remember. I couldn't help but listen, Glenna answered silently. Aloud she said, "Did you show up after being gone for ten years just to discuss my love life?"

Her mother raised her chin in a way that reminded Glenna of Crystal. "No. Curiosity brought me back. I heard the sanctuary was doing well, and I wanted to see for myself."

Glenna sighed, sagging into the chair. "We're doing better

than ever before. It's good you came, really. Would you like me to get Crystal? You should see her. You'd be proud of her. She's eighteen, graduated last year."

Her mother picked up the snapshot and traced her finger over Crystal's image. A shadow of emotion passed over her face, and Glenna wondered if it was remorse. The look was gone before she could be sure. Abruptly she set the photo back on Glenna's desk. "No, I don't think that's a good idea. Crystal will be better off not knowing I was here. I doubt she would even know me." The thought seemed to depress her— her shoulders slumped, and a frown turned her lips down. Then suddenly she straightened and pasted an overly cheerful smile on her face. It was a pitiful sight in Glenna's eyes.

"As a matter of fact, I thought I could sneak through here without seeing anyone. Silly me for trying." She straightened and moved toward the door.

Glenna knew their encounter was about to end and she would probably never see her mother again. Pain and regret shot through her simultaneously. She had so much she wanted to say, to ask. How could she leave with so much unfinished? "Mom!"

Her mother hesitated at the door. Her gaze was carefully shuttered as she turned back.

Glenna squared her shoulders. If not for herself, then she had to have answers for Crystal. "Mom, tell me one thing before you go."

"What is it?" she asked warily. She grew rigid as she waited for the question.

"Why did you do it? Why did you leave Crystal and me? We needed you."

Her mother was silent for many seconds, and Glenna wondered if she would get an answer. The only thing that gave her hope was that her mom was still in the office and hadn't walked out without a word. *Please, Lord, I have to know. Part of me has believed it was my fault. I know it was Dad and all his mistakes, but I need to know she didn't leave because of me, too.*

"Some people out there—emotional giants—can deal with anything. I'm not one of those people. I never was. But I think you are, Glenna. You can do anything you set your heart to."

It wasn't the answer she was looking for, but it was enough. Her mother turned the knob and jerked open the office door. On the other side stood Brent with his hand raised to knock. The stunned look on his face was almost comical as he looked at her mother, then at Glenna.

"Brent Parker?"

Brent lowered his hand, staring in bewilderment at Glenna's mom. "Yes, ma'am?"

"You stay away from my daughter, you hear me? Keep your distance, you criminal!"

Glenna wanted to cry out at the look of dismay that passed over Brent's face. Before she could protest, Brent had turned, mumbling something Glenna didn't hear. She wanted to chase after him and tell him to ignore her mom, but she blocked Glenna's path.

"How could you say that to him? He isn't a criminal!"

"You said yourself that he's like your father. Don't bother thanking me for the favor I just did you. In so many ways you're exactly like me, chasing after the wrong things."

"How can you possibly know what I chase after?"

Her mother ignored the question. "It's good I came when I did and prevented a disaster waiting to happen. You may not appreciate it now, but I saved you years of heartache."

"No! You *caused* me years of heartache. I have been so afraid I would be just like you. Every day I remind myself to stay away from Brent because if I love him, I'll be just like you and hurt the ones I care for most. Don't you think I'm scared you're right? I don't want to skip out when I'm desperately needed. I don't want to leave anyone behind as you did. But until that time comes I don't know if I'm made of tough enough stuff. I might be just like you. And that thought keeps me on my knees every day."

Her mother's cool blue eyes narrowed on Glenna's stricken, flushed face. She never had been nurturing, and Glenna didn't expect her to start now. Her mother made a helpless gesture with her hand. "You can thank me later." With that she stepped through the door and out of Glenna's life once more.

"How can I thank you?" Glenna cried bitterly. "Do you plan to leave a forwarding address this time?" There was no answer as she turned back to the shabby little office.

⋅⋅

Glenna found Brent in Veero's exhibit. He was standing over the pool, dropping bits of fish into the water. She wanted to cry out at the forlorn slump of his shoulders and the frown on his lips. His expression was grim as he stared at the white whale. Veero had no knowledge of Brent's mood as he happily slurped up the fish and chirped in appreciation. He was like a happy puppy, lapping up any attention Brent would throw his way.

"I knew I'd find you here. I think you'd sleep in here if you could," Glenna said, trying to keep things light to help him forget everything her mom had said. She climbed the stairs to the platform overlooking the whale's large pool. The icy water shimmered invitingly. Maybe someday she'd don a wetsuit with Brent and swim in Veero's tank. For now she was content to greet him from the edge.

Once beside Brent she knelt and gently slapped at the water

with her palm. Veero surfaced beneath her hand and sent out a fine spray of water.

"Do you think Veero gets lonely? Maybe we could find another beluga for him."

Brent didn't answer as he continued tossing pieces of fish into the water.

"Everyone is impressed with the remarkable turnaround the sanctuary has made since Veero's arrival. Even Keith Dempsen is surprised."

"Keith!" Brent snorted with disgust.

"I know you don't like him, Brent. But he won't be coming around here anymore." She hoped the words were true.

"I wish you'd stay away from him, but who am I to say? I'm just the hired help," Brent said with disgust.

Glenna didn't know how to answer since she hadn't seen him so upset. Usually he was the one teasing and bantering.

"Do you need a new job title? We could call you 'best friend of the month' rather than 'employee of the month.' Or maybe you just need a raise. More beach time, maybe?" Still Brent didn't answer, and Glenna realized her efforts at bantering were worthless. He didn't even acknowledge that he'd heard.

Glenna stared at his stony profile. She could tell by the set of his jaw that he was angry. Her idle conversation wasn't improving matters. Keith said she was a direct person, and he was right. It was best they got everything in the open. She breathed a quick prayer that God would help her smooth this over. She didn't like having Brent upset with her.

"That was my mother you met."

"So I gathered," Brent muttered.

"She had no business saying those things to you. I hope you didn't take them to heart."

Brent set the bucket at his feet and knelt beside Glenna.

He turned so he could gaze at her with eyes that seemed to look right into her soul. "Maybe she's right. Maybe it would be best if I kept away from you. You've dealt with your father's mistakes your entire life. There's no reason for you to be touched by mine."

"No! Your mistakes don't affect me. They were eggs! It's not you. I wish I could explain everything, but please believe it's not you."

Glenna wanted to make up for the hurt her mother's words had caused Brent. He didn't deserve that swift, brutal judgment any more than Glenna had deserved the years of punishment without a mother. Yet she didn't know where to begin. How could she explain to him that Mary Mayfield had reappeared after a ten-year absence only to bring more strife into Glenna's life? The wounds went deep, but the fear was even greater. She couldn't expect Brent to comprehend why she was so afraid to get close to him.

As she rose to leave, Brent's fingers closed around hers in a tight grip. She turned questioning eyes toward him, silently pleading for his understanding.

"You need to be free of this, Glenna—whatever it is. There are so many strings tying you to the past that you aren't free to enjoy the present. Do I make it harder for you, because of my prison record? If you want me to leave, I will."

The thought of losing Brent filled Glenna's heart with a dull, throbbing ache. Now that she'd found him, she wasn't ready to lose him. Neither was she ready to take the promises she read in his gaze. She was stuck somewhere in the middle and felt dry and empty because of it.

"If you left there would be no one—" She paused, feeling as if she was revealing too much of her heart when she couldn't promise him anything. In fact, she could offer him nothing.

She turned toward the small white whale and gave a helpless gesture with her hand.

"There would be no one to help take care of the animals?" His words were bland, but his gaze was sharp, challenging her to agree. They both knew he was more than just an employee.

"No, it's not the sanctuary!" she retorted.

"Then what? Tell me, Glenna. Why don't you want me to leave?"

"Because there would be no one to take care of me." And before he could question her further, Glenna scrambled to her feet and hurried away from the whale exhibit.

ten

Glenna, did you hear a word I said?" Keith asked with thinly disguised irritation.

Glenna returned his glare. "I thought I told you to send me a letter if you needed to tell me something. I wasn't joking when I said I would get a lawyer." She had too many things to work out, and Keith's unexpected appearance only complicated matters.

She'd been thinking about the fact that her mother was still there somewhere, wrecking everything in her path. Had Crystal seen her yet? She felt most concerned about Brent though. It was true he was more than her employee and had been for some time. He occupied her dreams as well as her waking hours and nearly every prayer. She wasn't sure exactly when it happened, but she was irrevocably, deeply in love with him. It was a hopeless situation. Love was supposed to be a joyous adventure, so why did she feel empty? Everything was complicated and growing more so by the hour. She wished she could have explained some of this to Brent, but it was impossible, and now Keith was here making everything more difficult.

"A man will mess with your mind and break your heart. Never fall for a con man." Her mother's words circled around in her mind until Glenna thought she would scream. It was too late. She'd already fallen for Brent, but she couldn't marry him or anyone else.

She'd never had any intention of marrying Keith though

he'd asked her to reconsider. It didn't make sense why he would want her for his wife when he obviously didn't love her.

Knowing he wanted to buy the property for Delta Ray was always tucked in the back of her mind, though he hadn't mentioned his company in some time. The only thing he ever talked about was her and their relationship. If he weren't so intent, the situation would be laughable. They had nothing in common. Again she wondered why a guy like Keith who liked fast cars and big parties would want her for his wife. There was no reason aside from the sanctuary. And there was no reason for her to consider his offer. He wasn't a believer, and they couldn't have a relationship. Not to mention that she didn't trust him. It was that simple. And she thought she'd made it clear the last time she saw him that *all* negotiations were over.

"I asked you if you've discussed my proposal with your father. I'm sure he'd help you see reason."

Glenna gave a sigh of frustration. Her father didn't like Keith or trust him. And as a Christian he'd never encourage her to marry an unbeliever. "No. And I'm too busy right now to meet with you. I have to figure out what to do with my mother." *If* there was anything she could do. The woman could still be walking around the sanctuary, or she could be halfway across the state. Glenna didn't know, and Keith wasn't helping matters.

Glenna sighed, feeling helpless. Brent was upset. And she had no idea where Crystal was. Glenna wanted to talk to her sister first in case she met up with their mom. It was bad enough that she couldn't get her mind off Brent and how much she loved him. Seeing her mother had put all her fears in motion. She never should have allowed herself to fall in love with Brent; yet how could she avoid it? He'd slipped past her defenses so easily.

Keith shifted in the seat across from Glenna's desk. His discomfort reminded her of her mother's visit and her condescending words about the office.

"Glenna, where are you? Will you listen?" Keith asked crossly. "I said I think you're making a big mistake."

This got Glenna's attention. *Mistake?* Refusing him had been the smartest thing she'd done.

Keith jumped to his feet. He circled her desk and bent over her until they were nearly nose to nose. Glenna shrank back, but he only leaned closer to her. "It's inevitable. We belong together. I've made up my mind, and nothing is going to stop me."

Glenna didn't have to pray to know Keith was wrong. They didn't belong together. She didn't even know what he believed in, besides the mighty American dollar. She laughed at the idiocy of his statement. "We don't belong together! Whatever game you're playing, Keith, it's time for it to end."

"It's no game, I assure you." His fingers bit firmly into her upper arms. "I think I've been very patient with you. Do you realize I've never asked another woman to marry me? Does that mean nothing to you?"

"Does the fact that I don't love you and you don't love me mean nothing to you?" she replied.

Keith straightened and shoved his fingers through his dark hair. For the first time he seemed flustered and unsure of himself. "What am I to do if you refuse? You have no idea how important this is to me."

"Then why don't you tell me what's really going on?"

Keith gave a sharp bark of laughter that held no humor. He turned his back on her to look out the window. Glenna doubted he saw anything of the beautiful view. And if he did, it probably meant little to him. He was normally so strong and self-assured. But today something was definitely wrong.

Dear Lord, You know I would help him if I could. Only You can give him peace. Help him see there is more to life than money.

"This little property you're sitting on is a gold mine, Glenna. I doubt you realize how much it's worth. The hotel I'm supposed to build here is an architectural marvel with every modern convenience imagined. But there's just one problem. I don't have a handle on the land yet. And if you don't sell it to me, then my job with Delta Ray Investments will be a thing of the past."

"What do your job and my property have to do with your marriage proposal?" Glenna asked, though she didn't need an answer. It didn't take a genius to figure out he was still trying to manipulate her. "You never liked me, did you, Keith? It was all part of the game."

Keith finally turned from the window and crossed back to Glenna. He took her hand and pulled her from the chair and unexpectedly into his arms. Glenna gasped and tried to push away, but he held her tight against his chest.

"You're right, Glenna. I won't lie to you. At first I saw you as a means to an end, and then you became a challenge. I couldn't allow you to rebuff me without trying to win you over. I've never met a woman immune to my many charms," he said with a self-deprecating chuckle.

"And now?" Glenna asked, though his answer had no bearing on her decision. She struggled to be free from his grasp, but his hold tightened.

"And now—I don't know. Somewhere along the way you got under my skin. I found myself thinking about you and wondering about you. I never expected to feel this way—sometimes frustrated, always intrigued. I think I have a crush on you."

"It sounds more like indigestion to me," Glenna said dryly,

trying again to free herself from his grasp. The longer he held her, the more uncomfortable she became.

"How can you treat this lightly?" he demanded fiercely. "I want to spend the rest of my life with you!"

Something didn't ring true with Keith's words. He appeared sincere as he gazed at her with his dark eyes, his lips mere inches from hers; but Glenna knew he didn't want her. It was just another desperate attempt to take the property. But the more she thought of Keith's motives, the less it made sense. The mammal sanctuary still belonged to her dad, so surely Keith knew he was trying to manipulate the wrong person. Unless something had changed that Glenna didn't know about.

Again she struggled against Keith's embrace, and he surprisingly let her go this time. She moved toward the door and held it wide so he could pass through. Keith remained where he was, glaring at her.

"This is because of Parker, isn't it? I never stood a chance."

"I don't know what you're talking about."

Keith took a threatening step toward her. "Don't you? What can he possibly offer you? I promised you a way out of this." His gesture took in the shabby office and piles of paperwork. "But you'd rather have him? He's nothing, Glenna. He'll hurt you, ruin the business, and leave you without two dimes to rub together. Do you want that kind of life?"

"I don't care what you say, Keith. Brent is a good, godly man. He'll rise far above what you say simply because of who he is. I care about him—and not you or Delta Ray can change that."

Keith stared at her in angry silence. His nostrils flared, and his fists balled at his sides. Glenna took a step back, concerned she'd pushed him too far. Yet she didn't regret a word she'd said. Brent was good, and she would champion him always.

Finally Keith forced a tight smile to his lips that resembled more of a grimace. "You'll be sorry you turned me down. I can be a formidable opponent, Glenna Mayfield. You better watch your step."

❧

Keith's threats rang in Glenna's mind as she went in search of her father. She hoped Keith wouldn't do anything more to harm the sanctuary, though it was likely he wasn't finished. Whatever the future held, she was glad she had stood strong against him. If she ever married, she would want the man God had chosen for her. He would be her spiritual leader, her best friend, her companion through thick and thin. She knew Keith could never fill that role.

Keith's actions raised a lot of questions in Glenna's mind about the sanctuary, and she knew only her father could answer them. Why did Keith come after her when her father owned the property? Or did he own it? Was it legally his free and clear, or were there mortgages she wasn't aware of? She doubted there was anything untoward with the financial standing since she handled all the bills. It would be difficult for her father to hide anything from her, and she doubted he would want to. Still, she didn't understand Keith's behavior, and it was high time to get some answers from her dad.

She found him at home, sitting on the sofa. He was staring fiercely at an old photo in one hand, a pair of scissors in the other hand. There was a pile of shredded letters and photos on the coffee table in front of him. His cheeks were damp.

"Did you see Mom?" Glenna knew he had. There was no other reason for him to bring out the old photos he hadn't seen in years.

"Yes," he muttered as he chopped at the picture. Tiny pieces dropped to the floor. "You'd think I'd finally get a clue after ten years and quit hoping she'd come back. I'm just a desperate old fool, holding tight to pipe dreams."

Glenna circled the sofa and sat close to her dad. Gently she removed the scissors and what was left of the photo from his hands. "You talked to her?"

"She told me in no uncertain terms she would rather die than put up with an old thief like me. I'm glad Crystal is spending the day with friends and was spared an ugly encounter. Mary told me she didn't want to see any of us." He sagged back against the sofa, looking defeated and older than she'd ever seen him.

"Oh, Dad, I'm sorry." Glenna didn't know how to respond—how to heal the wounds her mother had inflicted. Only God could comfort him, and she knew He would. God's love was like soothing oil as He touched all the parts that hurt. Seeing her dad's pain made her realize he was more wounded by her mother than by either her or Crystal. He'd been at a low point in his life when she left. And even after all these years she didn't have a kind word for him. Glenna couldn't help thinking they were better off without her mother and the destruction she caused.

"The wreckage of my marriage is walking around the exhibits with all those tourists, and I can't do anything to bring her back in."

The image of a damaged, dilapidated old boat came to mind and made Glenna smile. Her mother wouldn't appreciate being associated with a broken dinghy. "It looks as if there are two shipwrecks in the harbor," Glenna murmured. How ironic that both Keith and her mother were mingling in the same crowd.

"Brent?" her dad asked with a frown of concern.

"No, Dad, Keith."

Her father waved a dismissive hand. "Bah, Keith. He can't hurt us. Forget him. Brent is the one for you. He belongs here at the sanctuary. He's part of our family. Not Mary. Not Keith Dempsen."

Glenna shook her head, wishing she could make her dad understand. No matter how she felt for Brent or the feelings he had for her, they couldn't have a future together. Maybe God had brought him into her life, but she had to accept him as a friend and nothing more. Otherwise, she'd add years of suffering to them both. She couldn't take a chance that she was like her mother. She wouldn't make the mistake of loving him only to abandon him when he needed her most. Seeing her dad's desolation only furthered her resolve.

"I don't think so, Dad. I don't want to hurt Brent like Mom hurt you. Her blood runs through my veins as thickly as yours does. It's impossible."

Her father turned in his seat to stare at his daughter. "How can you say that?" He brushed at her short curls and tucked them behind her ear as he had when she was a child. For years she harbored bitterness against him and never allowed herself to know him. She was just beginning to see what a sensitive and gentle man he was. "You haven't turned into a thief because of my blood. What makes you think you'll be a deserter because of your mother's blood?"

For once Glenna didn't have a ready answer.

"Don't you see these things happened because of our choices and not because of heredity? My father and grandfather never spent a day behind bars. Mary's mother stood by her husband's side for fifty years."

"I want to believe this, Dad," Glenna whispered. She

pressed her eyes closed, afraid to let go of her self-made prison in case it came rushing back.

Trust, Glenna. Accept freedom. He who the Son made free is free indeed.

"You're nothing like your mother. She's as dry as the desert, but you, Glenna, you have riches of the heart. *You* didn't abandon me when I needed help the most. You patiently led me to the Lord's doorstep without ever turning your back on me, even when I deserved it. Mary chose to leave, but even as a little girl you chose to stay. My aunt wanted to take both you girls and raise you. Do you remember? But you wouldn't go with her. You valued me when I had no value. I know you'll never hurt Brent. You have too much love in your heart to give anything less."

"You don't think I'm like her?" Glenna whispered in disbelief. A glimmer of hope began to shine in her heart. Did she dare to believe him?

His fingers tightened over hers. "No, Glenna. You *never* were."

Riches of the heart. God had deposited them in her. She wasn't dry and empty as she'd believed, living in fear of who she might become.

"Really?"

"Really, honey. You are your own person with your own choices to make. I know I can trust you to make good ones."

Glenna clutched her dad in a bone-crushing embrace as the walls that held her for so long began to crumble. She was free! She was free to make her own choices. The shadow of her mother's desertion no longer clung to her like a bad omen of the future. "Dad, I have to find Brent! I have to tell him!"

❧

Brent sagged against the side of the fishing boat and sighed.

He was tired. After working all day at the mammal sanctuary, the last thing he wanted was to put in eight hours of back-breaking labor on the fishing boat. If they didn't locate the schools of fish quickly, it meant even longer hours. He didn't mind the smell of fish; he even liked pulling in a successful load. And when the truck dumped off a load of feed fish at the sanctuary, he knew it was all worth it. But he didn't like the rough crew he worked with. Cursing, drinking, lying, and cheating were commonplace with the men, and they knew Brent didn't fit in with them. They reminded him of the men he had done time with in prison—only now there were no bars. The sooner he was set free from this responsibility, the better. He needed to talk to Glenna.

Men shouted profanities around him as they readied the nets. Usually Brent helped, but tonight he couldn't bring himself to move from the bow of the boat. The waves rocked gently against the pier, the old wood creaking and groaning with every motion. He'd close his eyes, just for a moment.

"Hey, Parker! Get your lazy rear up! You got a visitor, and we need to shove off!"

Brent woke with a start and glanced around him in bewilderment. Two men stood over him with nets in their hands, glowering down at him.

"A visitor?" He scrambled to his feet only to sway unsteadily against the bow. Woody Sewler, the captain, glared at him. "Get off the boat, Parker. We're behind schedule tonight as it is. I'm docking your pay for this—you can count on it. Maybe we'll have room for you tomorrow. Maybe not."

Brent didn't know what was going on as he scrambled off the boat. As soon as he disembarked, men were at the ropes, casting off. The engines roared to life with Woody at the helm. He threw Brent a look of intense dislike as he pulled the boat away from the dock.

"Brent."

Brent turned to find Glenna standing behind him. Concern clutched his heart at the sight of her. She wouldn't be there unless something was wrong.

"I had no idea you were working two jobs. Why are you working for Woody Sewler?" she asked.

Brent knew he was dreaming. Nothing could look or sound as good as Glenna standing there, murmuring over him in concern. She was a vision for his tired eyes. Her dark curls were tousled by the strong breeze. Her blue eyes widened with worry as she stared at him. When she shivered and stuffed her hands deep into her pockets, Brent shrugged out of his jacket and dropped it around her shoulders.

"There was a little matter of getting feed fish for our animals. This was the easiest way to rectify the situation." He tried to keep his answer light, but Glenna saw through his efforts.

Tears filled her eyes as she stared up at his face. "You're doing this for me. Oh, Brent. I didn't know. You should have said something. I could have—"

He shook his head and waved away her protests. "It doesn't matter now. I probably don't have the job anymore since Woody Sewler isn't an easy man to work for. You weren't ever his girlfriend, were you?"

Glenna's somber expression gave way to a ready grin. "No! Did he tell you we dated? You didn't believe him, did you?"

"Not for a minute." Brent grasped her elbow and steered her down the swaying dock toward more solid ground. She leaned into him for support as they walked. "Tell me why you're here. Has something happened?" he asked, his concern returning.

"Dad told me you were here. I wanted to talk to you. I saw my mom."

"I know. I saw her, too. Remember?"

Glenna shook her head. "But you don't understand. I'm nothing like her. She left, but I didn't. I never saw this until now. I didn't leave. Don't you see?"

Try as he might, Brent couldn't untangle the jumble of Glenna's words. He led her to the waiting car, hoping to get a better explanation once they were out of the wind. She handed him the car keys, and after helping her into the passenger side, he slid behind the wheel.

"Now start over from the beginning," he said, turning in his seat to face her.

"Brent, look over there." She pointed toward the far shore, where the marine sanctuary was nestled against the beach. The sun was setting in the distance. An orange glow filled the horizon, melding with the setting sun. Purple clouds hovered around the building, pluming toward the sky. "Is that smoke I see mixing with those purple clouds?"

Brent stiffened, then frantically reached for the keys. "That's no cloud. The sanctuary is on fire!"

eleven

Brent tried not to break every speed limit driving the short distance back to the sanctuary. All the way he muttered prayers with Glenna's stiff "amens" punctuating every plea.

"Maybe it's nothing," she said.

"Yeah, maybe."

It seemed to take forever to reach their destination. As they got closer, the big black cloud hovering over the building grew larger. Their hopes that it wasn't the sanctuary vanished.

They screeched to a stop in the now-empty parking lot and rushed to the locked front gate. Brent waited impatiently for Glenna to punch in the security code. She seemed cool and collected, but he knew she was just as rattled as he was.

"I need to check on Dad! If the fire has spread to the house, he won't be able to get out."

"You go check on him, Glenna. I'll try to find the source of the fire. And go call the fire department!" He wanted to stay with her but knew time was of the essence. They could cover more ground if they split up. Brent muttered a quick prayer of safety over Glenna as he watched her dart away from him. Soon the thick billowing gray smoke swallowed her up. Losing her in the dark cloud caused him a moment of panic so strong that he almost went after her. But he forced himself to move in the opposite direction. He had to find the source of the fire and make sure no one was hurt.

The smoke was thickest and darkest near Veero's exhibit, causing fear to clutch him. He felt responsible for that little whale—swimming defenseless in his tank as the water temperature reached high levels. Crouching low and pulling his shirt over his nose, Brent made his way into the shadowy darkness. The smoke stung his eyes and burned his lungs. He tried not to breathe too deeply, taking shallow little breaths that still drew the smoke into his mouth and made him cough. He had to keep going. As he moved down the wide corridor, the smoke was so thick he couldn't see anything ahead of him. Water sprayed ineffectually from the random ceiling sprinklers over him—triggered by the smoke. The water ran off Brent's hair and soaked his shirt. He put his hand against the wall, allowing the smooth surface to guide him to Veero's tank. He could hear the whale making nervous little clicking sounds.

"It's all right, buddy," Brent called, hoping his familiar voice would reassure the animal. "We're going to get the fire put out. Hang tight."

The source of the fire wasn't anywhere near the whale's exhibit, so he crept back into the corridor on his hands and knees where the smoke wasn't as dense.

He fervently prayed Glenna was okay. What was he thinking, sending her off by herself? As he turned to go after her, a strange sound made him pause and listen. It sounded like someone pounding on one of the heavy metal doors. But which one? A half dozen doors lined this corridor alone, leading to different supply and machine rooms. The thought that it could be a guest or one of Glenna's family trapped spurred him on.

"Anyone there? Can you hear me?" he called as he passed each metal door. As he neared the last one a frantic tapping met his call. Brent tried to open the door, but it was locked.

"Just a minute! Hang on! I've got to get the keys." Why,

oh, why didn't he have them in his pocket this once? He was thankful a spare set was not too far away. Brent retraced his steps to one of the other metal doors and threw it open. The power was out, but he knew his way in the darkness. Across the examination room to the cool stainless steel counter he crept. He bumped a cart on his way, overturning a box of small tools that clattered to the floor. At the counter he felt for the right drawer. Not the first one under the sink. Not the one next to it, but the third. He was taking too long. He ripped the drawer open and fumbled for the keys, praying no one had used them and forgotten to replace them. No, they were there. His fist closed around the bunch of keys, and he hurried back the way he'd come.

Lord, let whoever's trapped in that room stay okay. Comfort him and protect him.

He was glad it wasn't Glenna. She wouldn't be in this wing of the sanctuary. Could it be Crystal? Brent tried to remember what she'd said her plans were. She prattled on and on about her social life. He prayed this was the night she was going out with her friends.

Brent reached the door again. "I've got the keys. Hang on a minute. Are you okay in there?" He tapped at the door. There was a soft tap in response. At least the person was still conscious.

He slipped one of the keys into the lock, but it wouldn't turn. He tried another and then another before finally getting the right one. At last the knob turned in his hand, and he forced the door open. Water from overhead sprinklers flowed into the corridor.

"Who's in here? Are you okay?" He stepped into the dark room. Cold water rushed over his feet up to his ankles.

Someone reached out and grasped Brent's shoulder. He

whirled around to see who it was but couldn't make out the man's features in the darkness.

"You gotta help me, Parker."

"Keith Dempsen? Is that you?"

"Yeah, it's me. Help me out of here, will you? The fire's just on the other side of this room."

Brent tried to make sense of what Keith was saying. There was another exit to the room. He hurried over to the door.

"Don't touch it!"

Wise warning. The metal door would be burning hot if the fire was truly on the other side as Keith said. Brent hurried back to Keith's side, sloshing through the water. There was too much water. The ceiling sprinklers hadn't been on that long.

"Did you do this?" Brent demanded.

"Do what? I didn't—start the fire, and I—I didn't bust any of your precious hoses. Help me out of here, Parker," Keith groaned.

"What's wrong with you?"

"I think I broke my leg. I was trying to force this door open, but I fell—slipped on all that water. It hurts a lot, and I can't stand on it." He coughed.

Brent looped his arm around Keith's waist and pulled him through the doorway. It wasn't easy with the water around their ankles and pouring from the sprinklers and smoke filling their lungs with every breath. Brent bent as low as possible while still supporting Keith.

"You're no lightweight," he said, grunting.

Keith coughed hard, nearly tumbling to the ground, but Brent held him upright. Slowly they made it down the corridor to the open lobby where the smoke wasn't as thick. A little farther and they'd be at the gate.

Brent lowered Keith to a bench inside the main entrance, away from the smoke and fire. As he straightened to go and find Glenna, Keith grasped his arm.

"You win, Parker."

"What are you talking about?" Brent demanded impatiently.

"You win Glenna. You ruined everything. How could I sweep her off her feet when she was always thinking about you?"

"So you try to burn down the sanctuary in revenge?" Brent shoved away Keith's hand. "I don't have time for this. I have to go find her."

⁊⋅

The closer Glenna got to her house only a few yards behind the sanctuary, the thicker the smoke became. When she came in full view of the house it was a shock. Smoke engulfed the entire dwelling, and orange flames licked at the front windows. She was too late to save the small home. She could only pray God would help her dad if he was still inside!

She circled around the back of the house, knowing it would be impossible to get through the front door. A constant prayer was on her lips as she pushed through the screen door. Smoke filled the house, and she couldn't see anything.

"Dad! Dad, are you in here?" she screamed. There was no answer. She wanted to believe he had gotten out safely, but something told her he was still inside. And she had to find him fast.

She dropped to her knees and crawled down the narrow hall that led to the family room. Bedrooms were on either side of the hall. "Dad!" she called, pausing in each doorway. He wouldn't be in her room or Crystal's. He was probably in his own room or the family room.

The smoke burned her eyes, so she squeezed them shut as she crawled, feeling her way down the hall. Deep coughs racked her body, but she knew she couldn't give up. "Dad!" she called from the doorway of his bedroom. Her voice wasn't strong. The smoke was making her throat ache and her voice scratchy. "Please, Dad, answer me!" Still no response. She choked on a cough that turned into a sob.

Lord, help me find him.

His room was empty. She frantically searched the bed and the floor in case he had passed out, but he wasn't in the room. She retraced her steps back into the hall and crawled toward the family room. The smoke was thicker, and she knew the flames were swallowing everything in their path. She had to reach her father before the fire did!

He wasn't on the sofa as she predicted. Instead she found him lying facedown on the floor in the middle of the room. His wheelchair was tipped over beside him.

"Oh, Dad, you tried to get out of here, didn't you?"

It took all Glenna's lagging strength to roll him over. She checked his pulse and was relieved to feel the steady beating at his throat.

Thank You, God. Thank You he's still alive! Please help us get out of here!

Glenna knew she wasn't strong enough to pull her father out of the burning house. The smoke was too thick, and they had no more air. A fit of deep coughs clutched her chest, and Glenna wondered if she'd ever be able to breathe normally again.

It was too hot in the house and growing hotter as the inferno consumed everything. She heard a loud crash, and Glenna knew part of the roof had given way to the flames. She had to get them out now! She grabbed her dad's wrists and dragged him several feet. His inert weight was too much. She'd never get him down the hall and out of the house in time.

"God, help me!" she croaked. Hot tears scalded her eyes and ran down her cheeks. She swiped at them in frustration.

Suddenly strong hands gripped her around the waist and lifted her to her feet.

"Brent!" She barely sounded the words, but he must have heard.

"Go!" He pointed toward the hall leading to the back door. Glenna waited long enough to watch him stoop and pick up her father. He grunted under the weight but remained steady as he lumbered down the hallway behind her and outside.

In the distance they could hear sirens approaching.

Brent carried Glenna's father down the path toward the beach, away from the burning buildings. Once they were many yards away and safe, he set him down in the sand. Glenna rushed to her dad's side, kneeling over him.

"Dad, can you hear me? Dad!"

A gash on his forehead was bleeding profusely. Glenna looked around for something to staunch the flow. Brent peeled off his wet outer shirt and handed it to her. When she touched the cold fabric to her dad's forehead, he groaned. The sound was the most precious utterance she'd ever heard!

"Thank You, Lord!" Brent exclaimed.

Her dad opened his eyes and peered up at his daughter. "You look worried, Glenny. What is it?"

He hadn't called her that in years. She could remember visiting him in prison and his admonishing her to take good care of everything. *"Watch after Crystal, Glenny. You're the best thing she's got. And take care of the dolphins since they love you most."*

"Dad, the sanctuary—our house, too—it's all burning to the ground. It's gone." Fresh tears filled her eyes and trailed down her dirty face. She clutched at his hand desperately, wishing he could make it better.

"Don't despair, Glenna. Have faith. It'll be okay. Right, Brent?" he asked, turning to the younger man.

Brent nodded in return. "I don't think anything can save the house, but the sanctuary is safe. It's not as bad as it seems. Even with all the smoke, the animal exhibits are safe. The entire front portion is clear. That's where I found Keith. I left him at the gate."

Glenna stiffened and stared at Brent, her gaze locking with his. "Keith is here?"

Was Keith responsible for the fire? He'd threatened her to watch her step when she refused his proposal of marriage. Had he done this to get even? One way or another he intended to take the property from her family, but she never expected he would do anything so drastic to acquire it. But then again Brent had accused him of tampering with the marine pumps. Would he stoop to setting fires?

"He's not going anywhere. He broke his leg."

This was unreal. "How did he do that?" she asked warily.

"It seems he was trying to escape the fire through one of the machine rooms. I have no idea what he was doing there in the first place. He didn't explain himself, and I didn't take the time to cross-examine him."

"Because you had to come and save me—and my dad." She pushed all thoughts of Keith and the fire from her mind as she gazed into Brent's eyes. She didn't know when he ceased being only her employee or only her friend. Now he was so important to her, as though he made up her missing part.

Yesterday these thoughts would have made her feel so helpless, but today she was free. She may be her mother's daughter, but she was made of sterner stuff. If Brent ever got into trouble again—and she prayed he wouldn't—she would be right there by his side. She would never abandon him when he needed her the most. His prison record didn't matter to her. She hadn't considered it for some time. It wasn't a part of who he was, just a side trip on the path he walked. No, neither of their pasts mattered—only their future together, if he would have her. Now that she had discovered the riches God had deposited in her heart, she didn't want to waste another second.

"Brent, I need to tell you something." She leaned forward, not caring that her dad could hear every word between her and Brent. He needed to know how much he'd grown to mean to her and that God had changed her heart. As she opened her mouth to tell him of her love, she noticed someone striding down the path toward them.

"What is it, sweetheart?" Brent asked gently when she faltered. He reached over and brushed a stray curl from her forehead. Glenna stiffened and stared past him at Keith, who was leading two police officers toward them. The police were here, but where was the fire department? Flames were consuming her home and business, and the police had come?

"This man—this *convict*—is the one who started the fire!" Keith called out.

As Brent and Glenna scrambled to their feet, the firemen and paramedics arrived. Glenna was momentarily distracted by the paramedics as they rushed to her father, asking questions. The firemen worked with frenzied haste to put out the fire. The scene was chaotic and overwhelming.

The two policemen approached Brent, one showing his badge. "We're not going to arrest you formally at this time, Mr. Parker, but we do have a few questions."

Glenna looked at her father, who seemed to be in good hands, then back at Brent. "This isn't right! You shouldn't have to tell them anything, Brent. You were with me!"

Brent shook his head, casually shrugging. Glenna knew he was anything but casual by the wary look in his eyes. "This is all part of having a record. I'm sure your father has gone through the same thing. Whenever something goes wrong, we're the first suspects. It's only natural." He turned to the officers, pressing a smile of resignation to his lips. He looked like a gladiator going into battle. But he wouldn't fight alone.

"Lord, I refuse to let him take the blame for something he didn't do. Help me think of the right words to say in his defense that won't make matters worse," she prayed under her breath. She turned, feeling Keith's gaze upon her, a triumphant sneer covering his handsome face. Glenna wanted to wipe the smirk from his lips. He thought he'd won— having Brent arrested, setting on fire the now-successful mammal sanctuary. All so he could acquire the land at a bargain-basement price for Delta Ray Investments. Well, he hadn't won yet. Glenna brushed past Keith to stand beside the policemen.

"I have a few questions of my own, Officer!" She deliberately turned toward Brent, her gaze locking with his. She saw uncertainty wavering in his eyes, but this was no time to reassure him. Lifting her chin and straightening her shoulders, she pointed at him. "I'd like to know how Brent Parker managed to start a fire when he was at the fishing docks with me."

No one said anything. Even the firemen's ruckus faded in the background.

"What about Mr. Dempsen's broken leg?" she asked, turning suddenly on Keith. "Didn't Brent have to help you out of the building because you were in too much pain to manage on your own?"

Still no one answered her questions. It didn't matter, because she had everyone's attention. "And why, Mr. Dempsen, were you trespassing on private property? No guests are allowed on the premises once the gates are closed. And yet you're here when an unexpected fire breaks out. Do you have any answers?" Glenna stepped forward, going toe-to-toe with Keith. She felt like the prosecuting attorney about to win her case. Fortunately for her she was much shorter than Keith, coming only up to his chest.

It was then she noticed the sheaf of papers tucked in his breast pocket. She snatched the papers before he could stop her. They were copies of financial reports from her office.

"You broke into my office and stole these reports! Officer, Brent Parker isn't the man you should be questioning. Brent was with me when the fire started and when this man, Keith Dempsen, was rifling through my office."

Keith tried to grab at the papers, but Glenna held them away. "Those aren't what you think, Glenna!" he growled. "This is all a huge misunderstanding. Quit playing around and give me the papers back. They're important documents for Delta Ray."

Glenna stepped closer to one of the policemen for support as she carefully unfolded the papers. They were Marine Mammal Sanctuary of Long Beach financial reports, exactly what she'd said they were. "Delta Ray has no business seeing these papers, Keith, and you had no right taking them. Was the fire a convenient cover that got out of hand, or did you really want to destroy the property?"

"I did not start the fire!" Keith barked. He shoved his hand through his hair in agitation.

"Why should we believe you? You tampered with the hoses on the dolphin tank and expected me to blame Brent. You cut off my feed supply by threatening Duke Sewler. Brent fixed that mess, too. You tried to get me to fall for a phony engagement. Admit it—you never wanted to marry me. You don't even like me. Why should I believe anything you say?"

"Glenna, I can explain—"

"You don't have a broken leg, do you, Keith?"

Keith shifted uncomfortably, avoiding her gaze, and Glenna knew everything she accused him of was true. It didn't hurt that he never cared for her. What hurt was that she'd been such a fool. She hadn't trusted him in the beginning. She never fancied herself in love with him or believed he felt any lasting affection for her. But she hadn't realized how dangerous he could be. He had to win, and he would do it at all costs. She should have been more cautious and never let things go this far.

"He didn't start the fire, Glenna."

"What?" She whirled to stare at her father in disbelief. How would he know what Keith had done? Her father pushed away the paramedics and struggled to sit up.

"He didn't start the fire."

Glenna rushed to her father's side and gripped his dirty, smoke-stained hand. His fingers felt limp within her grasp, and she was afraid he was hurt worse than she first suspected. He had a head wound and was mumbling gibberish. She gingerly touched the wide bandage the paramedics wrapped around his forehead. "Dad, are you thinking clearly? How do you know what Keith was doing? You were in the house when he was snooping around my office. How could you possibly know it wasn't him?"

Her father sadly shook his head as he reached up and pressed his palm against Glenna's cheek. His eyes held regret and so many emotions she couldn't identify. "I'm sorry, Glenny. So sorry."

"But why, Dad?" She squeezed his hand painfully, afraid to hear his answer, though she suspected what he was about to say.

"I'm the one who started the fire."

twelve

All in all, everything was back to normal, Brent mused as he tossed fish into Veero's tank. Of all the animals—the seals, the dolphins, the otters, and the walrus—he loved the little white whale best. Veero clicked and chirped contentedly, drawing his usual crowd of spectators.

Two months had passed since the fire. The investigation concluded the fire had started unintentionally as Glenna's father admitted, and he was free from further scrutiny. The Marine Mammal Sanctuary had to close briefly for renovations—mostly cosmetic. None of the animals or exhibitions had been damaged in any way. Brent knew it was because of God's perfect protection and thanked Him often. As He cared for the birds and flowers of the field, the Lord watched over every unique sea creature, as well, even those swimming in circles in a marine sanctuary.

They had flown in several specialists to monitor the animals for injury. Gary Erickson had come, as well. It was good to get his friend's approval of a job well done. He said he hadn't seen Veero so content and responding to his environment so well. He also mentioned, in teasing, that Brent seemed equally adapted to his environment.

When the doors reopened to the public, the tourists poured in. At first they came out of curiosity. The fire had become a local media event overnight. But when the novelty wore off, a steady stream of patrons still passed through, and it looked as if the sanctuary had risen out of its financial slump.

Brent knew Glenna was relieved to have the bills paid, with a considerable amount remaining each month from the vast donations and grants. They were even considering expansion, which wasn't pleasing news to Delta Ray Investments.

Even though Keith Dempsen hadn't started the fire, he admitted to all the other misdeeds Glenna had accused him of: breaking into her office and stealing reports, tampering with the hoses and pumps, shutting down her feed supply, and stealing medications. He didn't admit to using these tactics in all his business dealings, but it was enough to earn him a six-month prison sentence deemed by the courts—a decision he was currently appealing. Keith was no longer the top star with Delta Ray, but the corporation was still interested in the property. Brent wondered how long it would be before another executive was sent to try to persuade the Mayfields off their land.

The only thing that wasn't nicely tied up with a "happily ever after ending" was his relationship with Glenna. They were still on friendly terms, working closely together, attending church, and sharing most meals, but it seemed as if they were both holding their breath—waiting for something. Sometimes he would catch Glenna watching him with a wistful expression. He knew he looked the same way. More and more he knew he wanted Glenna for his wife and didn't want to wait—he loved her with all his heart—but he didn't know how to broach the subject without scaring her away. God had brought them together, and he didn't want to do anything to spoil things. The old Brent would have rushed forward, forsaking caution. The Brent of today couldn't do that. He wanted to build something lasting and knew any impatient move on his part could ruin it. So he waited, watched, and prayed for the right moment.

❧

Glenna didn't know what Brent was thinking or feeling, though she had her suspicions. But suspicions weren't enough when it came to relationships. She wanted to know for sure how he felt about her, because she was certain of her own feelings. She loved him and was no longer afraid to make a commitment to him. If anything, she was afraid he might slip away before she had a chance to tell him how much she cared. She didn't know why she hesitated. The past weeks had been busy with rebuilding the sanctuary and dealing with the publicity, but that wasn't why she held back. She was uncertain how to approach him. She couldn't simply walk up to him and tell him she wanted to spend the rest of her life with him. It didn't work that way.

And yet that's exactly what she was about to do.

Her dad had just dropped a bombshell in her lap when he told her his future plans for the sanctuary. Even now she had difficulty believing all that had transpired.

"I'm giving the mammal sanctuary to you now, Glenny. Crystal doesn't want it, and she's asked me to write her out of the agreement. She says she wants to take a different path with her life that has nothing to do with the coastal waters of Long Island. She's young, and she needs to explore what she wants from this life and seek out all the riches God has for her. But she knows her mind in this. She wants you to have the sanctuary, and I agree."

Glenna remained silent, not daring to interrupt her dad. She waited for him to continue, knowing something important was about to be revealed to her. She felt oddly nervous, though she didn't know why.

Her dad grasped her hand tightly as his intense gaze met hers. She studied his expression for any signs of fatigue but saw none. Even the cut above his brow was healed to a thin pink line.

"There's a stipulation, Glenna, and I'm serious," he continued, drawing her attention back to his words. "This place was never meant to be managed by one person. It takes a team."

Glenna nodded in agreement. "We've made a good team, Dad."

He shook his head. "No, I'm not part of your team anymore. And Crystal isn't on the team. But Brent is. Do you understand what I'm saying? He's a good man, and I know you love him. No, don't look so surprised. I have eyes in my head, and I see how you look at him. You don't have to say a word for me to know what you're thinking. I've thought long and hard on this decision, and I know it's the right one."

"What are you saying, Dad? What does this have to do with Brent and me?"

"I'm leaving the ownership of the sanctuary to you and your husband. All the papers are drawn up and ready to be signed. You just need the husband. You might think I'm being presumptuous, but I'm not. I really feel this is right."

When Glenna tried to interrupt, her father raised his hand, silencing her argument. "I won't have you growing old alone, breaking your back over this business. Not only is it a place of healing for weary sea creatures, it should be a sanctuary for human hearts. I always wanted that but never achieved it. But you've been successful where I've failed. Marry the man you love and continue this ministry to God's hurting creatures."

Glenna had left her father feeling stunned and overwhelmed. He thought he was doing the right thing by pushing her and Brent together, but how could she explain this to Brent? And what if he didn't want any part of her father's plan? It seemed her father had finally taken a leap off the deep end, and he was taking her and the mammal sanctuary with him. She could either marry Brent or lose everything she'd fought so hard for. It was true she loved Brent, but what if he didn't want her in return? She needed God to give her the right words now more than ever.

Lord, You set me free from all that worry and guilt. And I know You won't fail me now. Dad seems to think this is best, and in my heart I believe he's right. Please show me how to handle this, Lord.

Her silent prayer gave her courage as she searched for Brent. She loved him and needed to tell him.

She expected to find him hovering near Veero's tank, but he wasn't there. She searched all the exhibitions and finally found him sitting in the darkened observation room watching the harbor seals. Nervously she joined him on the bench, trying to formulate what she should say.

"We're getting some of that red algae over in the corner again." He pointed to the far corner of the tank where algae carpeted the smooth bottom. "I thought I had the pumps set right, but the current keeps missing that spot. I'll have to tamper with the water flow."

Glenna nodded absently, barely hearing him. "Brent, I have something to tell you, and it has to do with my mom. And the sanctuary, too. And my dad."

Brent didn't seem at all perplexed by her rush of words. He turned in his seat and gently grasped her hand. He interlaced his fingers with hers as he waited for her to continue.

Here it was. It was time to tell him she loved him and that she was no longer afraid of the future. She was free. "Brent, I just talked to my dad, and he has a frightfully strange plan for the sanctuary—and if I don't agree, he's going to sell. I want to keep the business, but he says I have to have a husband." She wanted to cringe as the words flew out of her mouth.

That wasn't what she'd meant to say at all!

Brent's gaze widened slightly, but he didn't so much as blink in response. "Run that by me again."

She needed to back up and start over before she made a total mess of it. Taking a deep breath, she started over—from the beginning. "Brent, you met my mother, remember? She always warned me to stay away from a man with a prison record because she was so miserable with my father. He always needed money but never obtained it honestly. He was in and out of jail more times than any family should have to bear. Her words hung in my mind years after she abandoned us. While I was raising Crystal, caring for my dad, and managing this business, my mother's words guided my every move. I realize now I listened more to her than the words I read in the Bible. I was so afraid I'd be like her, Brent. That's why I didn't want to get close to you. I was afraid that when times got tough I'd desert you the same way Mom left Dad."

"But you didn't leave, Glenna—remember? In Galveston you stepped up and defended me. You could have left or taken sides against me, but you didn't. And you stood by my side again when Dempsen tried to accuse me of starting the fire."

"Dad helped me see the truth. Finally I was set free from the guilt and worry that has bothered me all my life. I never wanted to hurt anyone the way I was hurt. I think that's why I worked so hard, to prove I wasn't like her. I can now see that Dad is right. God poured so many good things into me. I can rely on Him and trust in everything He gave me."

"Riches of the heart," Brent murmured.

Glenna nodded, remembering her dad had said the same thing. The words were like a confirmation from God. "I love you, Brent. And I'll always stand by you no matter what."

"I never had any doubts, sweetheart."

As Glenna leaned forward to kiss him, Brent pulled back. "Now tell me the part about needing a husband."

Warmth crept into Glenna's cheeks, and she wished she could avoid this part. She felt foolish for the way she had blurted it out earlier. Yet forging ahead, she briefly told him everything her dad said. The marine sanctuary needed a team to manage it, and her father planned to turn it over to Glenna and her husband. "I know this sounds crazy, but Dad is adamant about having his way."

"How can I be sure you really want me and not just the sanctuary?" Brent questioned.

"I told you I love you," Glenna answered in earnest. "And if you don't believe me, I'll tell Dad to sell the sanctuary." At Brent's look of surprise, she rushed on. "You mean more to me than this business ever could. I think Dad saw I needed a push to get my feelings out in the open. I've never been good at sharing the way I feel, but I'll try to change that. I don't care about the sanctuary, Brent. All I want is you. Is there anything more I can give you?"

"You can give me your promise." Brent moved to kneel before her, taking her hand in his. "Promise me you'll share those riches in your heart every day as we grow old together. Sanctuary or no sanctuary, I plan for us to be together always. You said you'll stay by my side. And I promise to cherish you and take care of you as you deserve."

He drew a tiny box from his pocket and opened it. Inside was nestled a beautiful diamond ring, more lovely than any she had ever seen. It wasn't as glamorous as the one Keith had presented, but this one suited her perfectly.

"You planned this!"

Brent gave her a sheepish smile. "Your offer of a mammal sanctuary is flattering, but I'd rather have just you. Say you'll marry me, Glenna, my love. I've made many mistakes, but that's in the past. Please share my future."

Glenna wrapped her arms around his neck, hugging him close. "You still get the sanctuary," she warned before he pressed a kiss to her lips.

"Whatever you say, boss," he said with a chuckle.

"Not boss—*partner*," she responded gladly.

❧

The wedding between Glenna Mayfield and Brent Parker took place in the dimly lit alcove beside the dolphin aquarium. It seemed the most obvious place for them to get married— they'd met at the sanctuary and invested so much of their time and energy there, and now their futures were forever tied with it. The marine sanctuary represented so much of what they both loved.

Candles gave the alcove a warm romantic glow, and flowers turned it into a fragrant tropical paradise. As Brent and Glenna exchanged their vows, staring lovingly into each other's eyes, the dolphins frolicked on the other side of the glass. The guests—Glenna's family, friends from church, Gary and Chloe, and even Brent's parents—smiled and whispered with delight as the dolphins darted, flipped, and dove as if in approval of the ceremony.

Once their pastor announced them to be husband and wife, Brent pulled his bride into his arms.

"Mrs. Parker," he said softly. With a triumphant gleam in his eyes, his lips took possession of hers. He continued to kiss her until all Glenna could think about was the love they shared.

It was a love God blessed them with when He brought them together. They were no longer two souls searching for freedom and fulfillment. They had both found what they needed in the riches God provided.

A Letter To Our Readers

Dear Reader:
In order that we might better contribute to your reading enjoyment, we would appreciate your taking a few minutes to respond to the following questions. We welcome your comments and read each form and letter we receive. When completed, please return to the following:

Fiction Editor
Heartsong Presents
PO Box 719
Uhrichsville, Ohio 44683

1. Did you enjoy reading *Riches of the Heart* by Tish Davis?
   ❑ Very much! I would like to see more books by this author!
   ❑ Moderately. I would have enjoyed it more if

   _____

   _____

   _____

2. Are you a member of **Heartsong Presents**? ❑ Yes ❑ No
   If no, where did you purchase this book? _____

   _____

3. How would you rate, on a scale from 1 (poor) to 5 (superior), the cover design? _____

4. On a scale from 1 (poor) to 10 (superior), please rate the following elements.

   ____ Heroine   ____ Plot
   ____ Hero   ____ Inspirational theme
   ____ Setting   ____ Secondary characters

5. These characters were special because? _____

_____

_____

6. How has this book inspired your life? _____

_____

_____

7. What settings would you like to see covered in future
   Heartsong Presents books? _____

_____

_____

8. What are some inspirational themes you would like to see
   treated in future books? _____

_____

_____

9. Would you be interested in reading other **Heartsong
   Presents** titles?   ❏ Yes   ❏ No

10. Please check your age range:
    ❏ Under 18   ❏ 18-24
    ❏ 25-34   ❏ 35-45
    ❏ 46-55   ❏ Over 55

Name _____

Occupation _____

Address _____

City, State, Zip _____

Hearts❤ng

Any 12
Heartsong
Presents titles
for only
$27.00*

CONTEMPORARY ROMANCE IS CHEAPER BY THE DOZEN!

Buy any assortment of twelve *Heartsong Presents* titles and save 25% off the already discounted price of $2.97 each!

*plus $2.00 shipping and handling per order and sales tax where applicable.

HEARTSONG PRESENTS TITLES AVAILABLE NOW:

Presents

Great Inspirational Romance at a Great Price!

Heartsong Presents books are inspirational romances in contemporary and historical settings, designed to give you an enjoyable, spirit-lifting reading experience. You can choose wonderfully written titles from some of today's best authors like Andrea Boeshaar, Wanda E. Brunstetter, Yvonne Lehman, Joyce Livingston, and many others.

When ordering quantities less than twelve, above titles are $2.97 each.
Not all titles may be available at time of order.